ABOUT THE AUTHOR

Maria Quirk Walsh began writing in 1988, after winning a Dublin Millenium short-story competition. She has had several stories published in magazines and won the *U Magazine*/Irish Mist short-story competition in 1993. *Searching for a Friend* was her first full-length work of fiction, and was short listed for the 1994 Bisto Book of the Year Award. *A Very Good Reason* is her second book for the Bright Sparks young adult series. She lives in Dublin and has one son and one daughter.

DEDICATION

For two very special people who never fail to
encourage me — my husband, Tommy, and my
mother, Jane Margaret Quirk.

PROLOGUE

The drive to the nursing home took about half an hour. Throughout the journey Laura Phelan sat in stony silence in the back of the car. In front, her parents chatted, but the fair-haired girl, her face unusually serious, refused to be drawn into their conversation. She'd hardly spoken to them at all during the past few days. In fact not since that evening when they'd mentioned the possibility of her Great-aunt going to live in a nursing home. During all the weeks the old lady had spent with the family since she'd been discharged from hospital, it had never occurred to Laura that something like this might happen. She hadn't given it a moment's thought, never imagining her parents would ever consider such a thing, especially where her Great-aunt was concerned and her mind was still reeling at the prospect. They'd always seemed so fond of Auntie M, so interested in her well-being. Yet here they were on their way to look over what, in Laura's opinion, was one of those terrible places. They knew she was completely against the idea. Her reaction to her parents' suggestion had left them in no doubt as to how she felt. Had they forgotten so quickly, she wondered, how whenever the Phelan family had any sort of problem or trouble her Great-aunt had always been there, ready to help in any way she could. And now,

5

it seemed to Laura, just when she needed them most they were prepared to desert her. However, despite her feelings about the whole thing, Laura had agreed to accompany them to see Milton House this afternoon — but for one reason only. If she couldn't prevent her parents from putting her Great-aunt into a home, at least she'd make sure that, at worst, it would be clean and comfortable.

It was a bright, sunny afternoon, but as they drove along, Laura saw none of the pleasant countryside through which they passed. She sat staring out of the window as it flashed by, her mind a million miles away. Her parents were silent now, too, as they watched for the turn off the main road onto the side road which would lead them to their destination. Minutes later it came into view and, slowing the car down, her Father turned onto it. A sign a little further on confirmed that they were heading in the right direction and soon they were turning in through the high wrought-iron gates of Milton House. The car crunched its way up the gravel, tree-lined driveway, coming to a halt opposite a flight of steps which led up to the front door of the stately Georgian mansion.

'Looks lovely from the outside, anyway,' Marjorie Phelan said to her husband, while casting a glance over her shoulder in her daughter's direction. Without replying, Laura opened the door of the car and, stepping out, looked all around her. Her eyes took in the well-cared-for grounds and the neat flowerbeds dotted here and there. A number of old people were strolling round the lawns, while others relaxed in deckchairs, taking advantage of the warm sunshine. The sound of laughter drew her attention

First published in Ireland in 1994 by
Attic Press
4 Upper Mount Street
Dublin 2

A catalogue record for this title is available from the British Library

ISBN 1 85594 135 X

The moral right of Maria Quirk Walsh to be identified as the author of this work is asserted.

Cover Design: Angela Clarke
Origination: Verbatim Typesetting and Design
Printing: Guernsey Press Co Ltd.

This book is published with the assistance of The Arts Council/An Chomhairle Ealaíon.

to one particular group who sat conspiratorily together in a sheltered corner. There was no way they could be residents, Laura decided quickly, noting their smiling faces. Nobody in their right mind, living permanently in such a place, could possibly find anything to look happy about! And, as her Mother and Father got out of the car, she reassured herself with the thought that the laughing group could only be visitors like themselves.

Laura followed her parents up the wide granite steps, standing apprehensively behind them as her Father pressed the bell. The huge mahogany door of Milton House was slightly ajar and, almost immediately, the sound of footsteps could be heard. Within seconds the door was thrown wide and they found themselves being greeted by a pleasant-faced middle-aged woman.

'Can I help you?'

'We've an appointment to see the Matron,' Laura's Father informed her. 'Phelan is the name.'

'Yes, of course. She's expecting you,' she told him as she gestured to the three of them to step inside.

Laura found herself standing in a large, square entrance hall. In the middle stood a highly polished octagonal-shaped table displaying a neatly arranged assortment of magazines and newspapers. An attractive floral arrangement sat in the centre. There were comfortable chairs placed around the walls, and through the stained-glass panel down either side of the hall door the afternoon sun streamed in giving the whole area a warm, welcoming appearance. She and her parents followed the woman across the hall and along a corridor off to the right. Halfway down she stopped and knocked on a door bearing the words 'Matron's Office'. Laura hesitated on the threshold as her parents entered the small room, but an attractive red-haired woman in a crisp white uniform beckoned to her to come in and indicated a chair. She sat down awkwardly as, shaking hands with her parents, the woman introduced herself.

'You found us without any trouble, I hope,' the Matron asked.

'None whatsoever,' Marjorie Phelan assured her.

'Good, good,' the red-haired woman nodded and then, her head tilted enquiringly to one side went on 'I believe you're here to discuss the possibility of your aunt coming to Milton?'

Over the next while her Mother and the Matron talked, discussing her Great-aunts condition, Laura's father interjecting with some comment every now and then. But although Laura didn't utter a word, all the time she listened intently to everything which was being said.

'Well now, perhaps you'd like to see the room we have vacant?,' the Matron suggested pleasantly when it seemed that the Phelan's had exhausted their list of questions.

'We would indeed,' agreed Laura's Mother.

'It's on the first floor,' the red-haired woman said and, ushering them out of her office, led them towards a broad stairway.

'What's that?' Laura spoke for the first time, pointing at what appeared to her to be some type of chair attached to the wall just below the first step.

'That? Oh that's for any of our residents who find it difficult to climb the stairs, my dear,' the Matron explained. 'You simply sit them in it, make sure they're securely strapped in, press this button and —

hey presto! they're on their way to the top'. She gave a light laugh as she saw the astonished look on Laura's face. 'We are here to look after them , you know. It wouldn't do to have them straining themselves now, would it?'

And not waiting for her to answer, with a quick stride the Matron headed up the stairs, immediately followed by Laura's parents. Behind them their daughter trailed slowly.

Again they found themselves being led along a corridor, a much longer, narrower one this time, at the end of which was an almost floor length window, obviously designed to let in as much light as possible. Today, it seemed to be living up to its architect's expectations, with a huge shaft of light reaching almost the length of the passageway. The Matron showed them into a room two doors from the end.

'This is it — one of our single occupancy rooms. You did say that was what you had in mind?' the Matron queried, turning to Marjorie Phelan.

'Oh yes. I've discussed it with my Aunt and she'd prefer a room to herself.'

'I can understand that, but, you know, single occupancy will cost her just that little bit more,' the Matron pointed out.

The room was bigger than Laura had expected and was attractively furnished. The single bed had a floral counterpane which matched the curtains, there was a good sized wardrobe, a washhand basin and mirror, and in one corner there was a small writing table with an armchair beside it. She watched as her parents looked around and then turned to each other with a nod of approval. Laura's heart sank, realising that the awful decision was one step nearer to being taken.

'The Dayroom is just along here,' the Matron was saying and once again the three of them followed her. Grudgingly, Laura had to admit that, like the bedroom she'd just seen, the Dayroom, too, was larger than she'd anticipated. It was also bright and welcoming and comfortably furnished with a TV in one corner. From the window where she now stood, there was a good view of the surrounding countryside and the grounds below. If it hadn't been for the thought of her Great-aunt having to spend the remainder of her days in a nursing home, at that particular moment Laura might just about have managed to admit that Milton House could, perhaps, prove to be a very pleasant place to live. As that very thought began to niggle uncomfortably at the back of her mind, hoping to find something she could criticise, she asked the Matron, somewhat rudely, 'Is this all there is to see?'

'No. We have another smaller room where residents can read in peace and quiet away from the distraction of television. But that reminds me,' the Matron broke off, turning to include Laura's parents in the conversation, 'I completely forgot to mention that your aunt could bring in her own TV and have it in her room, if she wished. It would give her that little bit more privacy and independence.'

'Hmmm, sounds like a good idea. And maybe her video, too,' Tom Phelan agreed. 'Then she could pick and choose whatever she wanted to watch.'

'Oh, and we organise a game of Bingo every Wednesday night for our residents, too,' the Matron added, 'and a hairdresser from one of the local salons comes in once a week for any of the ladies who wish to have their hair done.'

'Well, that seems to cover everything,' Tom Phelan said.

'No, there's just one other thing…' Laura's Mother hesitated.

'Yes, Mrs. Phelan?' The Matron waited.

'It's about bathing…You'll remember I mentioned that my aunt would find it impossible to manage getting in and out of the bath. I'd like to feel that…'

'That's no problem, no problem at all. We have the very latest in hoist equipment at Milton House,' the Matron assured her.

'Hoist equipment?' Laura looked questioningly at the Matron.

'Would you like to see?' she asked kindly, sensing a note of anxiety in the voice of the young girl beside her.

Laura hesitated for a second and then said, very definitely, 'Yes. Yes, I would.'

Taking her by the arm the woman led her towards a door a little further down which opened onto a large bathroom.

'That's a hoist,' she told her, pointing. 'We put our more infirm residents into it and lower them down into a nice warm bath. I know it may sound awful to someone as young and healthy as you, dear,' the matron said, as, her hand still on Laura's arm, she felt her stiffen, ' but I can assure you once they get used to it…'

But before she could finish Laura had pulled away from her and was pushing abruptly past her parents. The three adults looked after her in surprise as, without a word of explanation to any of them, she made her way hurriedly down the nearby staircase. She had to get out of this awful place. She couldn't bear to stay another minute, couldn't face being confronted with yet some other hideous mechanical contraption. Laura reached the bottom of the stairs and ran across the wide hallway, regardless of the curious looks from a number of old people who now sat there, taking a respite from the strong afternoon sunshine. Rushing out the door and down the steps she raced across to where her Father's car was parked, fighting to hold back her tears as she pulled the door open. But, once inside, they began to flow freely. She tried to shut out the picture which filled her mind, but failed. A picture in which she saw clearly her beloved Great-aunt in that dreadful thing, saw her being lowered down into water — like some trapped little animal about to be drowned. It was all she could think of. Over and over it flashed before her mind's eye and each time it seemed more terrible than the last. She'd never realised life could be so horrible. Why had all this got to happen? It just wasn't fair, she thought as, eyes red-rimmed, she gazed unhappily out of the car window and watched as her parents appeared in the doorway of the nursing home. They stood for a moment, deep in conversation, before slowly descending the steps.

Tom and Marjorie Phelan thought it best not to remark on their daughter's sudden exit, but when they'd driven a little way her Mother turned and asked 'Well, what did you think of the place, Laura?'

Laura couldn't bring herself to look at her and, avoiding her eyes, simply shrugged her shoulders. Marjorie Phelan sighed, but was determined not to give up too easily.

'It looked very well run to me. Your Father thought so too, didn't you, Tom?'

Her husband nodded in agreement. 'And the Matron seemed a kind person. Efficient, too, I'd say.'

But when Laura's only response was yet another shrug, her Mother turned away, her face sad.

Shoulders hunched, legs crossed, Laura sat on her bed, her diary balanced precariously on one knee. Her pen raced back and forth across the page, not easing up for a second, as though she was afraid her thoughts might escape her before she'd time to write them down.

"I can't believe what's happening. Suddenly my parents are like strangers to me. It's only a few hours since we visited that horrible place and already they're talking about selling 'Rosemount'. I overheard them discussing the cost of the nursing home just now when Dad said 'Two hundred and sixty pounds a week. Well, I suppose that was to be expected.' Two hundred and sixty pounds! Is that what it's going to cost? Who on earth could afford to pay out that amount of money — certainly not Mum and Dad. For a moment I thought everything was going to be alright, that Auntie M wouldn't be going there after all. But then Mum spoke. She reminded Dad that the Matron had said there were a few people interested in the vacancy, that they'd have to let her know within the next week if they were going to take it up and added 'that means the bungalow will have to go on the market immediately'.

The bungalow! Not 'Rosemount' surely, I thought, I can't be hearing properly. But I was, because next thing Mum said 'I'll really be sad to see 'Rosemount' go,' and my worst fears had been confirmed.

I couldn't bear to listen to any more. I crept quietly upstairs, thankful that at least Emma wasn't here. The last person I'd want for company right now is my nosey sister.

How could they even think of selling it. How could they talk about it so matter-of-factly? Mum would be 'sad' to see it go. That was all. Doesn't she remember all the good times we've had there? All those noisy, happy Christmases, the long summer days and weekends Emma and I stayed over. It's more than just somewhere to visit — it's a second home. I can't bear to think of some other family living there, of not being able to go over any more. I'd like to rush downstairs and burst in on their conversation, to tell them 'You can't sell it. Not 'Rosemount'. I won't let you.' I'd like to shatter their cold reasoning as to what should or should not be done.

Why can't they just leave Auntie M where she is? Why can't she simply stay here with us until she's well enough to go back to her own home? If they sell 'Rosemount' what then? She won't even have a home to go to. Sometimes I think I hate this world. Everything's so different and complicated all of a sudden. The past weeks have been like some terrible dream I can't wake up from..."

Laura paused for a moment from her frantic scribbling and chewing on the tip of her pen, sat staring into space, remembering...

CHAPTER ONE

The shuttlecock whizzed through the air. The girl across the net from Laura hadn't a hope of returning the service. It was what Laura's friends called one of her "specials".

'Fourteen — twelve. Matchpoint,' the umpire called as Laura changed places with her partner, Aishling. Taking careful aim, she served again — a short, sharp shot which dropped just inside the yellow line of the court opposite, catching her opponent completely off guard.

'That's it,' the coach announced, smiling at the four girls. 'If you all continue playing like that we should definitely make it to the finals this year.'

'Yessss!' the group of white-clad figures chorused, as they simultaneously tossed their badminton racquets high into the air.

'Watch it, you lot,' Deirdre O'Brien cautioned good humouredly. ' I don't want any of you injured before we even have reason to celebrate.

The girls laughed.

'And don't forget. Practise again on Friday,' she reminded them as they headed to the changing rooms.

'You really hit some brilliant shots today, Laura,' Aishling Dalton said as the two girls changed into their tracksuits. 'Coming for a coke to cool off?'

'Sorry, can't.' Laura's reply was muffled as she pulled the top of her suit over her head. 'I've got to rush over to Auntie M's. I promised I'd cut the grass for her today. I'd just love a coke, but I didn't expect the last match to go on for so long and I'm already late as it is.'

Mary Andrews, or Auntie M as she was affectionately known within the Phelan family, was Laura's Great-aunt. Aishling had met the handsome, grey-haired woman on numerous occasions when she'd visited the Phelan household and several times she'd accompanied Laura on her visits to her Great-aunt's home. The first time she'd met her , Aishling had admitted to her friend afterwards that she'd been expecting 'Somebody...well...sort of ancient!'

'Yeah, she really doesn't look her age, does she?' Laura had said that day, a note of pride in her voice. 'I don't know exactly how old she is, although I suspect she's about seventy. But you'd never get Auntie M's real age out of her. She says there are two things she doesn't discuss. One is her age and the other her bank balance!'

Aishling smiled to herself as she zipped up her sweatshirt, remembering a more recent meeting with Mrs. Andrews. She and Laura had been discussing their current favourite pop group when she'd joined in their conversation saying 'So that's the latest is it? Great, they're not bad at all!'

'Your Aunt's really a scream, Laura,' Aishling said now. 'Remember the day she came the whole way to Cork to cheer us on? She shouted louder than Ms O'Brien that day!' Aishling sounded so serious that Laura had to laugh.

'Yeah, she's terrific all right, and so full of life. She's always involved in something or other. If she's not playing bridge she's doing flower arrangements, or setting up a committee for some sale of work. Mum and I don't know where she finds the energy for it all. I've always admired her and I love going to visit her. You know, I can talk to her about anything.'

Listening to her friend, it was obvious to Aishling just how fond Laura was of her aunt.

'Right then, I'm off for a coke anyway,' Aishling said, picking up her racquet and slinging her sports bag over her shoulder. 'Sure you haven't time?'

'Sure.'

'Don't work too hard then.'

'I won't. See you tomorrow,' Laura replied, smiling.

For a woman of her age, Mary Andrews led an extremely busy, active life. But, no matter what came up, she always kept Wednesday afternoons free. Hail, rain or snow, Laura came over to see her on Wednesday, her half day from school. The young girl reminded her so much of what her Mother, Marjorie, had been like at the same age. She was a kind, thoughtful girl and Mary Andrews looked forward immensely to their afternoons together. But now that she was a teenager , she sometimes wondered if she wouldn't soon tire of spending her free time with someone so much older than herself. On this particular Wednesday afternoon, as she stood beside the window waiting for her to arrive, she hoped that if ever she did it wouldn't be for a very long time. She looked across now to where a sepia-coloured postcard stood propped against the mantlepiece. It showed a 1930s scene of Dublin's O'Connell Street. She'd picked it up a few days ago at a stall in the South Great George's Street Arcade and she hoped Laura would like it. Another one to add to her growing collection, Mary Andrews thought fondly.

Glancing at her watch, she saw it was after four o'clock and wondered what was keeping Laura today. She was usually so punctual. The sun had taken on a watery look and she noticed that quite a few clouds had appeared in what had earlier been a clear blue sky. She hoped it wouldn't rain before they'd a chance to get the lawn finished.

'Maybe I should get started on it, just in case,' she mused, considering the idea for a moment, not liking the look of the weather. Then deciding not to wait any longer, she headed out into the garden.

It was about a fifteen-minute bicycle ride from Laura's home to 'Rosemount', the large comfortable bungalow in which her Great-aunt lived. 'Rosemount' had been Laura's Mother's home, too, from early childhood until she'd married. When Marjorie Phelan had been about four years old both of her parents had been tragically killed in a car crash leaving her and her young brother, John, orphans. At the time of the accident, Mary Andrews, Marjorie's dead Mother's sister, had been married for several years but she and her husband were still childless and, having given up all hope of ever having children, they had been only too willing to take the two young orphans into their home and bring them up as their own.

Anxious to get to her Great-aunt's as quickly as possible, Laura took the shorter route — 'the back road' as the local residents called it. It took her down a country road, shaded on one side by huge old trees while the other was bordered by the lush fields of a stud farm. In one of them Laura could see a number of beautiful chestnut horses, roaming freely. Casting a glance to the right of them, as she rode along, her eyes took in the nearby riding stables. She'd had a few lessons there, but far too few for her liking. Riding lessons were expensive and she knew her parents couldn't afford them on a regular basis. But if she had one wish it was to learn to ride properly and maybe some day even own a horse of her own. Last year Auntie M had arranged for her to have a course of lessons as a birthday present and Emma, whose birthday was within days of her older sister's, had decided she'd like to learn too. Laura smiled now as she remembered their first lesson. She'd been given Dusty, a placid, gentle creature while Emma had had a jet black horse named Midnight. Emma and her mount had seemed to take an instant dislike to each other and, afterwards as they'd walked home together, still smarting from how Midnight had treated her, Emma had announced that one lesson was quite enough for her. To Laura's delight, their Great-aunt had agreed that she could avail of the remainder of Emma's lessons and she'd spent a few wonderful weeks with Dusty. Pity it had to come to an end, Laura thought now as she sped along, her shoulder length blonde hair blowing a little in the gentle breeze, some of it slightly damp after the strenuous badminton session she'd just had. But her green eyes soon began to sparkle as she thought of what Ms O'Brien had said at the end of this afternoon's practice. Wouldn't it be great if she and Aishling made it to the final of the North County Schools Championships. Last year they'd both been on the school's 'B' team. But this year they'd made it onto the coveted 'A' team and had been practising very hard ever since. It wasn't easy keeping up to 'A' team level. She and Aishling had been made very conscious of that this afternoon when they'd played against two other girls who had already been on it for some time. It had taken everything they'd got in them to win that last game. Still, she couldn't wait to tell Auntie M about their chances. She was always so interested in everything she did. Laura was looking forward, too, to seeing the postcard her Great-aunt had bought for her. She was really into collecting them now and usually came across one or two when she and Auntie M went on what Emma called their 'boring Sunday afternoon outings!' But Laura didn't find them in the least bit boring. It was Auntie M who had first awakened her interest in 'old things' as Laura described them. When she'd been about eleven, she'd taken Laura to the Antiques Fair in the Royal Hospital at Kilmainham and ever since Laura had loved browsing through antique stalls, consulting with her Great-aunt over this trinket or that. Every few weeks they went along to the Round Room of the Mansion House to see what the dealers had on display. Not that Laura bought much, apart from her postcards. But Auntie M quite often made a purchase, mostly things for 'Rosemount', but every so often something special for Laura, too.

Taking one hand off the handlebars of her bike, for just an instant, she patted the pocket of her tracksuit jacket, checking to feel if Nicole's letter was still there. Nicole was Laura's French penfriend. She lived in Marseille and the two girls had been corresponding with each other for almost four years. To Laura's delight, a few weeks ago her Great-aunt had suggested that if Nicole's parents were agreeable, and would allow their daughter take the train to Paris, she'd treat herself and Laura to a weekend there during the coming summer and then the two penfriends could finally meet. Nicole's letter today brought the reply that her parents were quite happy with the idea and that there was 'pas de problem'. So now it was only a question of settling on dates, and making the necessary hotel and flight arrangements! Laura was filled with excitement about the whole thing and couldn't get to 'Rosemount' fast enough. She and her Great-aunt had a lot of work and a lot of planning to do over the next few hours. She'd a feeling it was going to be a pretty hectic afternoon!

Laura arrived breathless at the front gate. A look at her watch told her that she was more than half an hour later than planned and hurrying up the garden path, she propped her bike against the wall beneath the livingroom window and rang the door bell loudly. Getting no reply, she rang again, this time peering in through the letterbox to see if her Great-aunt was coming. Strange, Laura thought when there was no sign of her. She knew I was coming over. She decided to try the back door, and headed round the side of the house, finding the tall wooden side-entrance gate locked as usual. Laura climbed up and, leaning over the top, stretched as far down as she could until her fingers reached the metal bolt. It slipped back easily at a push and she hopped down gingerly as the gate swung open.

The sight which met her eyes when she walked into the back garden made Laura stop short. Her Great-aunt was lying on the grass, the lawnmower toppled over on its side, right next to her crumpled figure. The shocked girl raced across the lawn and, going down on her knees, stared in disbelief at the unconscious woman. Her eyes were closed, and her face, deathly pale, looked somewhat different. As she bent closer, Laura realised that the righthand side of it was slightly twisted as though it had been tilted upwards.

Trembling Laura gently touched the still figure on the shoulder.

'Auntie M, Auntie M,' she said softly. But Mary Andrews neither moved nor spoke.

'Auntie M, it's me, Laura,' she said again, this time raising her voice a little. But there was still no response. Laura looked around helplessly, not knowing what to do next. She turned once again to look down at her Great-aunt and it was then that she noticed the large gash on the other side of the old woman's forehead. It was obvious she'd struck her head against the lawnmower as she'd fallen.

With a cry, Laura got up and ran into the house through the already open back door and going immediately to the phone in the hall, she began dialling frantically.

'Hurry, please hurry, Mum,' she implored as she

listened to the ringing at the other end of the line. After what seemed an eternity, she heard her Mother's voice and between sobs, Laura blurted out what had happened.

'Oh, Mum, I don't know what to do. She's just lying there...'

'Don't try to move her, love. Get a blanket and put it over her to keep her warm. Then go in next door and see if Mrs O'Sullivan is there. She'll stay with you. OK?'

When Laura didn't answer at once, Marjorie Phelan asked sharply 'Laura, are you all right? Are you listening, Laura?'

'Yes, yes, I'm all right. I know what you want me to do'.

'Good. In the meantime, I'll phone for an ambulance. Then I'll drive over straight away.'

'OK Mum.'

Her face streaked with tears, Laura replaced the receiver. She stood beside the phone for a second or two as though frozen to the spot. Then remembering what her Mother had said about a blanket, she raced into the bedroom and pulled the heavy cover from the bed.

Mrs O'Sullivan was out.

Why couldn't she be in today of all days, Laura thought. Despairingly she looked up and down the deserted road. There was no one else to call on for help. The next house was quite a long way up and Laura wasn't even sure who lived in it. Anyway, it was too risky to leave Auntie M alone for the length

23

of time it would take her to get there — especially if she found there was no one at home there either. The best thing to do, she decided, hurrying quickly back to where her Great-aunt lay, was to stay close by her until help arrived.

'Why didn't she wait until I got there? Why did she have to start pushing that heavy lawnmower around without me?'

Laura asked the same question over and over. Patiently, her Father gave the answer he'd already given her several times during the last few hours.

'She must have thought you weren't coming, Laura. That's probably what it was.'

'But, she knows I always come when I say I will. I never let her down, Dad.'

'I know, I know, love. But we'll never know exactly what happened until Auntie M is well enough to tell us herself. Now, it's about time we all went to bed. It's pretty late and your Mother's exhausted after all those hours sitting around in the hospital,' Tom Phelan said looking over at his wife who sat across the kitchen table from him and Laura, their younger daughter, Emma, having already gone to bed. Marjorie Phelan looked completely drained after the events of the afternoon. Her aunt had still been unconscious when the ambulance reached the hospital and there'd been no change in her condition when she left her bedside a short time ago. The doctor had explained gently that the old lady had suffered a stroke and, it appeared from the few tests they'd been able to carry out so far, that the righthand side of her body was completely paralys-ed. It was possible that she might regain some feeling over the next few days, maybe even a complete return, but, he'd stressed, there could be no guarantees at this stage. The medical staff didn't yet know if her speech would be affected, but, according to the doctor, strokes effecting the righthand side of the body carried a greater chance that it might be. It was a matter of waiting until she regained conscious-ness before they'd be able to tell exactly how bad her aunt's condition was. In the meantime, they'd stitched the wound on her forehead and made her as comfortable as possible

Although shocked herself by the news, Marjorie Phelan had managed to relay, as gently as possible to her daughter, exactly what the doctor had told her. She knew how close Laura was to her Great-aunt and how upset she'd been by all that had happened. When she'd arrived at 'Rosemount' just moments after the ambulance, she'd found Laura almost hysterical as she watched the ambulance men lift the still form inside the vehicle. She'd hardly had time to calm her before climbing in herself, the doors quickly closing behind her.

'When can I see her, Mum?' Laura wanted to know now.

'As soon as the doctor says it's OK. But for the present, he thinks I should be the only one to visit her.'

'But why?'

'Because he thinks it's for the best.'

'But, Mum....'

'Look, Laura,' her Mother said wearily, overcome now with tiredness, 'at the moment she wouldn't even know that you were there.'

Too upset to speak, Laura stood up from the table and quietly left the kitchen.

CHAPTER TWO

As soon as Aishling saw Laura in school next day, she knew something was wrong.

'Paralysed on one side!' Aishling repeated after Laura had told her the bad news.

'Yes. If only I hadn't been delayed at badminton it wouldn't have happened,' Laura said.

'Don't say that, Laura.'

'But it's the truth, Aishling. Pushing that lawn-mower was too much for her. I know it was. It brought on her stroke. It did, it did,' she insisted as Aishling tried to persuade her that she was wrong.

Laura was on the verge of tears as she spoke and, noticing the dark circles beneath her eyes, Aishling guessed she hadn't had much sleep the night before. She'd probably lay awake all night blaming herself for what had happened. She put her arm around her friend, and said 'Come on, Laura. You know it wasn't your fault. You were always helping your aunt. Don't blame yourself. Of all people, your Auntie M wouldn't want you to do that.'

But Aishling was wasting her time. Laura wouldn't be consoled and when the time came for them to go into class together, she was still in the same tearful mood.

When Mary Andrews regained consciousness, it was

immediately obvious that her speech had been effected. Her words were slurred and jumbled and , although the nursing staff were extremely kind and patient with her, she became agitated each time she failed to make herself understood. Now, several days later, there was still no sign of any feeling returning to the righthand side of her body and Marjorie Phelan had been told that her aunt would have to commence manipulative therapies as soon as she was strong enough.

'These therapies include physiotherapy and relaxation techniques, Mrs Phelan,' the Ward Sister informed Laura's Mother one afternoon. 'It's important that all stroke victims start them as soon as possible. It gives them the very best chance of a full recovery.'

'And her speech. Will they be able to do anything about that?,' Marjorie Phelan asked anxiously.

'Everything possible will be done,' the Ward Sister assured her. 'She'll have speech therapy every morning.

'Will she make a full recovery, do you think?'

'Well, she's a strong woman for her age. Determined, too, I'd say — from what little I've seen of her. But, of course, we'll just have to see how she responds.'

It was a week before Laura was allowed visit the hospital. At first when she saw her Great-aunt she hardly recognised her. She'd lost an enormous amount of weight. Her Mother had warned that she'd find quite a change in her and had wanted Laura to delay her visit until later that evening when her parents would be visiting, too. But Laura simply hadn't been able to wait until then. She'd been so anxious to see her that she'd taken the bus over to St. Michael's as soon as school was over. Could anyone have changed so much in just one week, she wondered as she looked down at the frail figure in the bed, knowing now what her Mother had been trying to prepare her for.

'Hello, Auntie M,' she said gently, bending to kiss her on the cheek.

The old lady mumbled something. Laura thought it sounded like 'Hello Dear,' but couldn't be sure. She forced herself to keep a smile on her face as her Great-aunt made some more unintelligible sounds, but although she tried hard, Laura found it impossible to hold a conversation with her. She wasn't sure whether she should be answering 'yes' or 'no' to whatever it was she was trying to say and as the visiting time moved slowly on, the strain began to tell on both of them until, eventually, all attempts at talk between Great-aunt and niece finally dried up.

'Yours,' Aishling called to Laura. But if Laura heard her partner, she didn't pay any heed to her warning and missed the shot completely.

'Laura, what's the matter with you?' Aishling hissed without even looking in her friend's direction, careful not to take her eyes off the girl opposite who was about to serve again, this time to Aishling herself. She knew she had to get the service back to their side of the court as soon as possible. She and Laura were already four points down and, although it was still the early stages of the championships, if they lost this match they probably wouldn't even make it to the quarter finals let alone the finals! So far today Aishling had had to play almost single-handedly since they'd come on court. Laura's mind seemed to be miles away and she was missing one shot after the other. Aishling smashed hard now as the shuttlecock came within her reach and felt a huge surge of satisfaction when she saw the surprised look on the faces of the girls on the other team. Now it was her turn to serve and, concentrating hard, she played like she'd never played before, determined not to let them think that she and Laura were a push-over.

'Well, that was close,' Deirdre O'Brien commented afterwards as a glum Laura and an exhausted Aishling flopped down onto a bench in the changing room. They'd won, but only just.

'You can say that again,' Aishling said, looking enquiringly at Laura, waiting for some explanation of her terrible performance. Laura sat with her head bent, fumbling with the laces of her runners.

'Sorry,' was all she mumbled, not offering any excuse.

'What's the problem, Laura? Girls on the "B" team play better than you did today even on their worst days. Weren't you feeling well, or something?'

The coach waited for the blonde-haired girl to reply. When she didn't, Deirdre O'Brien said 'I heard you've had a bit of an upset in your family recently. Aishling was telling me what happened to your Mother's aunt.'

Laura nodded, her eyes brimming.

'I don't want to sound harsh, Laura. But it's not going to help either you or your aunt if you spend all your time moping about. I'm sure she's getting the best of attention where she is at the moment and from what Aishling told me of the type of person she is, she wouldn't want you worrying so much about her. And there's the rest of the team to think about too, you know,' the coach added gently.

Laura looked up at her anxiously.

'There are lots of girls who are very keen to get a place on the 'A' team. If you keep on playing the way you played today, Laura...well, I've got to be fair to everyone, as I'm sure you understand.'

Laura understood only too well what Deirdre O'Brien was hinting at. If her performance didn't improve, she was out.

As she and Aishling walked home together, they hardly spoke. Laura's thoughts were on what their coach had said. She didn't want to lose her place on the team. She and Aishling had worked so hard to get this far. They knew each other's every move and played exceptionally well together — or had until today, she thought ruefully. She didn't want all their hard work to go to waste, yet it wasn't so easy to put Auntie M out of her mind. She just couldn't help thinking of her lying in that hospital bed. And always at the back of her mind was the thought that, somehow, she'd helped put her there. At night she lay for hours, unable to sleep, filled with guilt as she thought about what had happened. If only her badminton match hadn't gone on so long that day, things would be so different. Her Aunt would still be the healthy, active person she'd been a little more than a week ago. And now she found herself facing a second problem — the possibility that she might lose her place on the team. It seemed to Laura, as she trudged silently alongside Aishling, that she was somehow caught up in a vicious circle of unhappy events from which there seemed to be no escape.

Aishling, on the other hand, could have found a lot to talk about, but decided it was better to keep quiet just now. These last few days Laura had been pretty snappy with her. Only the other morning when she'd asked her if she was going to the weekly disco, she'd replied sharply 'You know I'll be visiting the hospital'. When Aishling had pointed out that the disco didn't start until half past eight and that people would still be going in around nine o'clock, Laura had almost bitten the head off her saying 'Look. I told you I won't be going. Right?' Aishling knew it was because she was so upset about what had happened to Mrs Andrews. Still, it hurt her when Laura behaved like that. She hoped things would sort themselves out as soon as the news about Laura's relative was more positive. For the present, she'd just have to be patient. Laura was far too good a friend to lose.

Laura accompanied her Mother on her visits to the hospital as often as she could. Her Aunt was gradually regaining some of her strength and was now having physiotherapy every day. She'd also started speech therapy, but her progress was slow and it was still difficult to understand what she was saying.

'We can't expect overnight miracles, Mrs Phelan,' the Ward Sister had said when Laura's Mother mentioned that she didn't see very much change in her aunt's condition. 'These things take time.'

Of course, Marjorie Phelan knew that the Ward Sister was right, that things couldn't be rushed. But her heart ached to see her aunt as she was now, confined for long hours to bed, her only change of scene being when she was taken elsewhere in the hospital for therapy. Marjorie was worried, too, about what the future held. She felt completely responsible for her aunt, who'd been widowed a number of years ago, and who had, apart from her, her husband, Tom, and the girls, no other close relatives. There was her brother, John, of course. But he was living with his family in England and only came home occasionally on holidays. It really left her the only person her aunt could turn to for help. Of course she'd give it willingly, she promised silently as she stood for a moment in the hospital corridor before going into the ward across from her. After all, Auntie M had been a mother to her when her own parents had died so tragically. Still, it was a worry. What if her aunt's condition didn't improve at all. Would she be able to give her the care she'd need? Would she be able to look after her, and two lively daughters and a busy husband? Would she? At this moment, depressed by her aunt's lack of progress, she just wasn't sure.

Laura, too, looked anxiously for some improvement in the old lady every time she visited her, but could see none. She couldn't manage to move around on her own. She needed either two nurses to help her, or had to be pushed about in a wheelchair. Like her Mother, Laura couldn't help but worry and wonder what would happen in the weeks ahead.

CHAPTER THREE

'Pity about your trip,' Laura's Mother said one evening as the two of them were driving home from the hospital.

'Yes. Nicole was really disappointed, too, from what she wrote in her letter,' Laura told her. 'But maybe when Auntie M is better we could go then,' she added hopefully.

'I wouldn't bank on it, if I were you, love,' her Mother warned.

Laura sat in disappointed silence.

'And you know,' Marjorie Phelan went on, 'despite Auntie M's condition, I don't think they'll keep her in the hospital very much longer.'

'You mean she'll be going home soon,' Laura exclaimed. 'Did they say when, Mum?'

'No — but reading between the lines of what the doctor said this evening, I don't think it'll be too long.'

'But that's great. We'd better get over to "Rosemount" and start airing the place,' Laura spoke excitedly, her face lighting up at the thought of having her Great-aunt back in her own home again.

'Oh Laura, don't be silly,' her Mother admonished. 'How on earth can she go back to 'Rosemount'. The poor woman can't even walk, never mind take care of herself.'

'But you said…'

'I said the hospital won't keep her much longer. Hospitals don't nowadays, you know. Not with all these health cuts. People are turfed out as quickly as possible, sometimes even before they're up to it, if you ask me,' her Mother said, a note of anger creeping into her voice. 'No, when she's discharged she'll have to come to stay with us. For a while anyway.'

'But that's brilliant, Mum. That means we won't have to worry or wonder how she's getting on. We'll have her right there with us. She can share my room. She can…'

Marjorie Phelan cut in on her excited chatter.

'It may not be as simple as it sounds, Laura. No, wait. Let me finish,' she said as her daughter opened her mouth to interrupt. 'If Auntie M comes to us, she's going to need a lot of looking after, and I mean a lot. It's going to be like having a baby in the house again, only adult size.'

Laura smiled at her Mother's description, but her expression quickly became serious when she said, 'There's nothing to smile about, Laura. It won't be easy and I'm not even sure I'll be able to manage it. But for the moment I just can't think of anything else except to have her with us to begin with. After that, we'll just have to wait and see how things work out.'

Once again Laura was silent.

She'd never heard her Mother talk like this before. She was usually so positive in her approach to things. It was strange to see her filled with doubt. And doubt about something as simple as having Auntie M home to stay for a while. As far as Laura was concerned, coming home from hospital was exactly what was needed to bring about her full recovery. She'd be right as rain in no time once she got back into familiar surroundings. And if her Mother had any doubts about the whole thing, Laura certainly had none.

When they got home Laura could talk of nothing else.

'Don't get too excited,' her Father warned, seeing how elated she was. 'They haven't said anything definite yet, you know.'

But Laura wasn't to be cautioned and ran upstairs to tell her sister the good news.

Even Emma, who never seemed all that interested in anything very much outside her own little 'bubble,' as Laura called it, appeared happy at the prospect of Auntie M's imminent discharge.

Later that night Laura lay in bed still thinking about what her Mother had said. Despite Marjorie Phelan's forebodings about how things might work out, her daughter felt happier than she'd felt for a long time. The past weeks had been the worst in her life. For as long as she could remember, Auntie M had been a huge part of it and she didn't know what she'd have done if she had died. It had been touch and go those first few days after she'd had her stroke. It was only when she had finally been moved out of the intensive care unit that Laura had begun to believe she might actually pull through. But then there'd been that awful setback. When her blood pressure, which, according to the doctors had been the original cause of the stroke, had suddenly shot up again…

But that was all in the past now, she told herself happily. Auntie M would be home soon. She'd do everything she could to help her get back to her old self. Her Mum would soon be convinced that there was no reason to worry about taking care of her. No reason at all.

As Marjorie Phelan had anticipated, within a matter of days the medical team at St. Michael's decided the hospital had done all it could and her aunt was declared well enough to be discharged. The Ward Sister had just been on the phone to say the family could take the patient home whenever it was convenient.

'Saturday afternoon? Yes, that'll be fine. We'll have her ready,' she'd said briskly, not wasting any further time on unnecessary conversation.

The problem of where her aunt would sleep now had to be decided, her niece thought as she replaced the receiver. The sooner it was sorted out the better. It would mean moving the girls about a bit. And she knew that one of them wasn't going to be too pleased!

'My room?' her younger daughter exclaimed when she broached the subject. 'Why can't she go in with Laura?'

'It'll be better all round if she goes into your room, Emma'.

'But why would it be better?'

'Well, Auntie M could be restless at night. I don't want Laura's sleep disturbed. She's got a lot of extra study this year and she needs a proper night's rest.

'But Mum,' Emma protested, 'couldn't you try

putting her in Laura's room first and see how things go?'

'I could, but I don't think it would work out. And it wouldn't be very fair to her now, would it, Emma, if we begin by shifting her around from one room to the other. She's been through enough these past weeks as it is.'

'Suppose not,' Emma said, her expression sulky. 'Oh, all right then,' she agreed grudgingly. 'But I want exactly half the space in Laura's wardrobe. She'd not going to make me push my things into some pokey little corner of it'.

Marjorie sighed as Emma headed upstairs to set about moving her things. It was amazing that two sisters could be so different. Emma had always been headstrong and obstinate while Laura was so easygoing and agreeable. Yet, on this occasion, she could understand her younger daughter's reluctance to agree. She knew that at Emma's age she'd have hated the thought of giving up her room, too. But there was no other way she could work things out. And besides, the smaller bedroom was nearest to the bathroom and with Auntie M's condition being what it was, the more convenient everything was, the easier things would be.

The following Saturday began warm and overcast, but as the day progressed the sun finally broke through. A good omen, Laura thought as she stood at the garden gate, watching impatiently for the car to turn the corner. She'd wanted to go to the hospital with her parents but they'd decided that it would be better if she didn't. Most of the back seat would be taken up with Auntie M's things, and with still no feeling in her leg, they thought she'd probably need more than the usual amount of space to stretch out. Her parents could have arranged for her to be driven in the ambulance, but Marjorie and Tom had felt that the journey home in the family car, although not necessarily more comfortable, would probably be more pleasant.

As she waited, Laura glanced back towards the house. Still no sign of Emma.

How on earth could she sit inside and calmly look at television at a time like this? she wondered. She'd never understand her sister for as long as she lived, she thought, still watching anxiously for her Great-aunt's arrival. At that moment she saw Aishling and her father walking up the road towards the house. Aishling's Dad had offered to come along and lend a hand, thinking Tom Phelan might need some help in carrying the old lady upstairs. Although she weighed little enough at the moment and he could have managed to carry her quite easily on his own, her parents hadn't liked to refuse Brian Dalton's kind offer of help.

'Not here yet, I see,' he commented as he and Aishling reached the gate.

Laura smiled.

'No. But any moment now, I hope.'

As she spoke the familiar car rounded the corner.

'Emma, Emma, they're here,' she called excitedly.

Laura rushed to open the door of the car as soon as it stopped, while behind her, finally making an appearance, Emma strolled leisurely down the garden path.

Brian Dalton swung a wheelchair out of the boot and, applying pressure to a handle at the base, had it ready and waiting in seconds for his neighbour's aunt to be lifted into it.

'Oh, it's so good to have you back home,' Laura said bending down and giving her Great-aunt a huge hug, as her Father gently deposited her into the chair. The old lady watched fondly as her niece made sure she was properly secured and smiled as she heard her ask 'Can I wheel her in?'

At a nod from her Mother, Laura began to carefully push the wheelchair in the direction of the house. As they made their way up the garden path, she glanced down at the frail figure in her care. Her heart was bursting with happiness. She could hardly believe her Great-aunt was actually home at last. She'll soon get well now, she thought silently, her head full with ideas as to how she could help her make a complete recovery.

'You're in Emma's room,' Laura told her Great-aunt as they reached the hall door. 'We've moved in together,' she went on, speaking over the top of her head, looking beseechingly at her sister, hoping she wouldn't say anything which would prove upsetting. To her relief, for once Emma seemed to have the sense to keep her mouth shut.

Later, having helped settle her Great-aunt comfortably in bed, and while her parents and Brian Dalton were chatting in the kitchen, Aishling and Laura headed off up to her bedroom. Even though Emma had only moved in two nights before, there was already an air of disorder about it.

'Not in its usual spick and span condition, is it?'

Aishling commented, familiar with the room and knowing how tidy Laura usually was.

'No, and all the indications are that it'll get worse,' Laura rolled her eyes to heaven in mock despair. 'But at the moment, I don't care about anything, Aishling. Just so long as Auntie M is home at last.'

Within a few hours, however, the first shadow was cast over Laura's happy mood. Just as the family was finishing their evening meal, her Mother looked at her and Emma and said, very seriously, 'Girls, I want you both to listen carefully to what I have to say'.

She'd left the hospital that afternoon, her head swimming with instructions from the matron and nursing staff. Now she had to pass on some of this information to the two girls sitting across the table from her. Laura waited, ready to hear whatever it was her mother had to tell them. But, as usual, Emma appeared to be only half listening, her mind obviously on something which she considered far more important.

'Emma.' Her mother spoke sharply, finally catching her attention

'There're a few things you both need to know about your Great-aunt's condition. The hospital think there isn't going to be very much, if any, improvement in her arm or leg. They don't think her speech will become much clearer either. The Speech Therapist gave me these,' she said, holding out a number of cards, each one with a different word printed on it. 'She suggested that when Auntie M finds difficulty with a particular word, she should show us these. It'll make it easier for us to understand what it is she wants to say…' Marjorie Phelan's voice broke slightly and for a moment she couldn't continue.

Seeing that his wife was upset, Tom Phelan taking off his glasses, rubbed his eyes wearily and picked up where she'd left off.

'They told us, too, that she'll have mood swings. You could go into the bedroom and find her smiling and happy one minute, and then, within a short time, she could suffer a bout of depression and begin crying for no apparent reason.'

He put up his hand to silence Laura, who was about to say something.

'It's important that you're both aware of these things. I know it's upsetting, but it's best that you have some idea of how it may be over the next weeks or months,' their Father told them.

Laura, who'd been so anxious to speak only a second or two before, now said nothing. The thought of her aunt having to make herself understood by holding out cards was something she couldn't even begin to imagine. Auntie M who'd never had any difficulty in expressing her opinions and putting her point across, who up to a few years ago had been a member of Toastmasters and had spoken before an audience on many occasions, was now expected to use word cards! Laura eyes filled with tears. She couldn't look at the other members of her family. She just sat there, her head bent.

'There's also the question of keeping up her morale. The hospital mentioned how important that is, too.' Laura's mother joined in the conversation again, now more composed. 'Things like helping her keep up her appearance. You know how particular she's always been about how she looks.'

Emma spoke unexpectedly, surprising them all.

'Maybe someone from the local hairdressing salon might come and do her hair for her sometimes, Mum,' she suggested.

'Well, there'd certainly be no harm in finding out,' her mother agreed, grateful that Emma, of all people, had managed to grasp some of what she'd been saying.

'Good idea, Emma,' her Father said quietly, glancing across to where his other daughter sat, still not saying a word.

CHAPTER 4

Over the following weeks it seemed to Marjorie Phelan that not only had her aunt come to live under the same roof, but that a whole group of people had moved in with her! There never seemed to be a quiet moment in the day. As soon as she managed to get the family out in the mornings, she began attending to her, bringing her breakfast, helping her wash, freshening up the bed, tidying up the bedroom and then, almost immediately, would come the first knock at the door. Sometimes it was the Physiotherapist. Other times it was the Speech Therapist. The District Nurse called every week, too, and each Friday a young woman who'd been assigned by her, came to help Laura's Mother give her aunt a proper bath. There'd also been a visit from the Occupational Therapist. The mobile stylist called on Saturdays to do the old lady's hair and there'd even been a visit from one of the local clergy. Sunday afternoons, too, always brought a stream of visitors. Mrs O'Sullivan drove over regularly. Auntie M's bridge partners called, as did old friends from Toastmasters and various other neighbours from round and about 'Rosemount' — the list was endless. Mary Andrew's niece had never been busier, had never had so little time to do so much.

During her visits, the Physiotherapist showed her

how to carry out a number of passive exercises which Marjorie was to do for her aunt on the days in between the therapists visits. The District Nurse arranged for a bed rest and pulley for the patient, emphasising how important it was that she be able to move herself around in the bed.

'The pulley will be of enormous help, Mrs. Phelan. Your aunt should be put as little as possible on her paralysed side. Lying too much on that side will increase the chances of bedsores developing,' she explained. 'With the pulley she should be able to manage to shift around quite a bit by herself . And it will save you a lot of backstrain,' the District Nurse had added kindly.

Laura and Emma had stared at the strange piece of equipment harnessed to the back of the bed, eyeing suspiciously the strap which hung down from the middle of it over their Great-aunt's head.

But it was the arrival of a commode which had really shocked the two of them. Getting Auntie M to the bathroom had proved an enormous problem. Very soon after her discharge from hospital Marjorie began to understand exactly what the District Nurse meant by 'backstrain'. In the evenings when Laura was around, between the two of them they somehow managed to manoeuvre the old lady from the bedroom, along the landing and into the bathroom. But during the earlier part of the day, when she had no one to help her, it was an almost impossible task. Her aunt was a dead weight as she leaned against her for support and more than once she thought she wasn't going to be able to prevent herself from letting her fall.

'What's that?'

Emma had been the first to speak when she saw the commode beside the bed. Seeing her aunt's eyes following Emma's pointing finger, her Mother had ushered her out of the room, explaining quietly what it was as they went downstairs.

'Ugh, it sounds awful. Imagine having to use something like that,' Emma wrinkled her nose in disgust as she spoke.

'Ssshhhh!' Laura hissed, as she came down the stairs behind them, pointing back towards the open door of the bedroom. 'Will you ever cop on, Emma? Don't let Auntie M hear you talking like that. You don't think she likes the idea of it either, do you?'

Laura paused, wondering how best she could explain to Aishling what she meant. The two friends were on their way to the badminton team's regular pick up point.

'Passive exercises are...well, you see, if someone isn't moving around much, or is confined to bed for a long while, like Auntie M, they could develop fallen arches.

'Really, Nurse Phelan,' Aishling smiled at her friend as she spoke. 'You know, you're getting to be a real expert on these things'.

Laura burst out laughing

This was more like the old Laura, Aishling thought, listening to her. It was amazing the difference in her friend since her Great-aunt had come out of hospital, she thought, as she waited for her to explain further.

'So, you exercise their feet for them every day by moving them in different directions.'

'You mean they just sit there and you do all the

work?'

'Something like that.'

'Interesting,' Aishling said and then 'Gosh Laura, look at the time. Come on, we'd better hurry'. The two girls immediately quickened their step. If there was one thing their Coach didn't like, it was being kept waiting. So for the rest of the way neither of them spoke, concentrating only on getting to the meeting place on time. It wouldn't help to be late and not have enough time for a proper warm up before the game began. Today's match was an important one. If they won this they would only have to get through one more before reaching the semi-finals.

'We can do it,' Laura whispered to Aishling a short time later as they were about to play for service. Aishling winked back at her, feeling equally confident . Now that her partner was back to her old self, she knew Laura would more than play her part. Thank goodness, she thought, as she prepared to take the shot, that Mrs Andrews was out of hospital at last!

After some weeks it became obvious that Mary Andrews was making very little progress. Her diction had improved only slightly and the Speech Therapist felt from her experience with other stroke victims, that there was very little else she could do for her patient. Sadly, she informed Laura's Mother she'd only be coming for a few more sessions. The righthand side of her aunt's body showed no sign of improvement either and now, as Marjorie sat on the end of the bed, gently exercising one of the old lady's feet, her spirits suddenly sank. She felt more tired than usual today. She still had her aunt's other foot to exercise, but feeling weary of the whole thing she decided that she'd leave it and ask Laura to finish the task when she got in from school. If it hadn't been for the help Laura had given these past weeks she didn't think she'd have been able to cope with all the extra work involved in taking care of Auntie M. She'd been terrific, learning how to do the various exercises, taking trays up to her Great-aunt at mealtimes, spending hours with her, keeping her company — even writing down what she tried to say in reply to her nephew John's letters from London.

'I'll send Laura up as soon as she gets in. She'll have you feeling on top of the world in no time,' she told her with feigned cheerfulness, as she settled her back comfortably against the pillows. But as she turned away from the frail figure in the bed , she knew that only a miracle could bring about any great improvement in her aunt now.

The sound of sobbing came from the bedroom. It wasn't the first time Laura had heard it. It had started when the Speech Therapist had stopped coming. Auntie M had taken the news very badly, seeing it as an indication that, as far as her speech was concerned, she couldn't hope for any further improvement. When, a short time later, the physiotherapist had announced that she wouldn't be coming very much longer either, the old lady had been extremely upset. For days afterwards she'd hardly spoken and had sat for hours on end simply staring into space. It had been difficult, too, to get her to eat, with her Mother actually having to feed her on a number of occasions. Dr. Nolan, the family doctor, had been called in and had prescribed some tablets in an attempt to lift her depression. But so far they didn't seem to have made very much difference. She was still extremely depressed, at times lying in bed sobbing just as she was doing now. Laura stood outside the bedroom door, uncertain what to do. The last time she'd heard Auntie M crying, she'd gone in to her immediately only to find that her presence had seemed to upset the old lady even more. She hadn't known what to do then and she didn't know what to do now. It used to be so easy to talk to her. But these days she didn't seem interested in anything. Not even the other day, when she'd come home and run upstairs excitedly with the news that the team were finally through to the semi-finals. She'd hardly said a word. Laura wasn't even sure if her Great-aunt had actually understood what she'd been talking about.

She gave a troubled sigh and decided that she'd better go downstairs and tell her Mother what was happening. She found her in the kitchen surrounded by a pile of bed linen, something which seemed to have multiplied since Auntie M's arrival.

'Mum.'

What is it love?'

'She's crying again.'

'I'll go up,' her Mother said getting up wearily. 'You know, Laura, things aren't going to improve. Your Father and I have been...Oh, look, I'll talk to you later,' she said, leaving her daughter mystified as to what she'd been about to say.

* * *

'But you can't.'

Laura stared at her parents, her green eyes filled with disbelief.

'You can't be serious about putting Auntie M into one of those terrible places.'

Emma sat on the sofa beside her, but appeared to be only half listening, as usual. Laura knew it was no good looking to her for support, conscious of her glance every few seconds in the direction of the television screen across the room. Although the sound had been turned down — so they 'could talk' as her Father had put it — Emma still couldn't seem to take her eyes off it.

'They're not terrible places,' her Mother said defensively. 'Most nursing homes are extremely well run.'

'Well, I don't believe that. The truth is that you don't care about her. You just don't care,' Laura said angrily.

'Don't be ridiculous. Of course we do,' Tom Phelan told his daughter firmly. Both he and his wife had known Laura would be upset at the news, but neither of them had expected her to react quite as strongly as this.

'You don't think we'd put her into any old place, do you?' he asked. 'Your Mother and I have been making some enquiries during the past while, if you must know, and we've managed to get the names of some very reputable homes. As it happens, we're going to look at one of them on Sunday. You can come with us and see for yourself what it's like, if you want.'

Laura said nothing.

'Look, love. Don't you realise, we've no choice,' her Mother spoke gently, seeing the stricken look on her daughter's face. 'I've looked after Auntie M since she had her stroke. She can't make it to the toilet, she has difficulty in communicating her needs, and on her good days she can just about feed herself. And she's getting worse instead of better, can't you see that? Soon she'll have to have everything done for her, and now with all this crying...well, I just can't cope any more.' Abruptly, Marjorie Phelan burst into tears. Laura hated it when her Mother cried and she seemed to be doing an awful lot of it lately. With an impatient toss of her head, she got up from the sofa and stormed out of the room...

Still chewing on her pen tip, Laura slowly drifted back to the present as she became aware of the sound of her sister's voice from the hall below. She glanced warily towards the door, half-expecting Emma to come rushing in at any moment. Quickly, she snapped shut her diary and deftly turned the key in its tiny lock.

CHAPTER 5

'I thought all the awful things which could happen had happened already,' Laura said dismally to Aishling as they walked to school together. 'First Auntie M's stroke, then all the talk about Milton House. And now this.'

'Are you absolutely sure they're going to sell it?'

'Absolutely. My mother was on the phone to my Uncle John last night. Remember I told you he lives in England. Well, I heard her asking him to come over next weekend, if he could, to discuss how they're going to go about the sale.'

'Does your aunt know yet?'

'I don't think so. But she probably suspects. Anyway, if she hasn't enough savings to pay for the nursing home, then selling the place is the only way they can come up with the money. So, one way or another, in the end she'll have to be told. After all, the bungalow is hers and no one can sell it without her agreement.'

'Suppose you're right,' Aishling said. 'But maybe your uncle will have some other ideas. He may feel the same as you. Maybe he won't want the place sold either. Maybe he'll even persuade your Mother to change her mind about the nursing home.'

'That's really what I'm hoping for.'

Both girls were silent for a moment, Aishling thinking how she'd hate anything like this to be happening to someone in her own family.

'I can't imagine anyone else living at 'Rosemount,' Aishling. Auntie M was so much part of the place.'

'Yeah, I know what you mean,' her friend agreed quietly, remembering the times they'd gone there together.

* * *

'Laura's taking the whole thing very badly,' Marjorie Phelan said to Sheelagh Dalton, refilling her coffee cup as they sat companionably together in the kitchen. 'We couldn't get a word out of her yesterday on the way home from visiting the nursing home. She seems to have shut Tom and I out completely.'

'You haven't told her yet, then?'

'No, I can't. It's far too soon. And anyway, anything could happen at this stage...'

Aishling Dalton's Mother smiled sympathetically.

'As far as Laura's concerned, I can't wait to get rid of Auntie M as quickly as possible,' Marjorie sighed.

'Try not to worry too much, Marge. It won't do you any good at the moment. And anyway, you know what they're like at that age — everything's either black or white. No matter what anyone tells her, she'll think she's got it right! I'm sure it'll all work out in the end.'

'I hope so. I'm sure I'd have managed to look after my aunt for much longer under normal circumstances, but with the way things have happened...'

'I know. I know'. It was all Sheelagh Dalton could think to say and she patted her neighbour's hand affectionately, feeling totally inadequate as she saw the distressed look in the other woman's eyes.

* * *

Laura hardly recognised her room when she arrived home that evening. Since Emma had moved in with her it had been nothing but a mess, but today was really the last straw. There were clothes everywhere! Some were hanging over the wardrobe door, others thrown carelessly across the back of the dressing table chair and, oblivious to the state the room was in, her sister lay sprawled on top of whatever else had been left lying untidily on her bed.

'Emma,' Laura shouted, trying to make herself heard over the noise of the ghettoblaster on the bedside locker beside the younger girl. Although her sister was only two years younger, sometimes Laura felt as if they'd been born decades apart.

'Emma,' she shouted even louder as she reached out to switch off the offending piece of equipment. 'What do you think you're doing with that thing blaring like that?'

Her sister looked up at her with innocent blue eyes.

'Listening to it, of course.'

'Don't be so smart. I know you're listening to it, but did you ever think that Auntie M might not want to listen to it, too. She must be deafened,' Laura said angrily. 'And look at the state of this room. It's unbe-lievable.'

'Look at this room. Look at this room. That's all you ever say to me. You're always on at me about it. What's wrong with it anyway?' Emma asked, glancing around her.

'What's wrong with it? Everything's everywhere, that's what's wrong with it,' Laura told her sister angrily.

Heatedly Emma hit back, 'I wish I'd never had to share with you. I wish I was back in my own room.'

'Keep your voice down. Auntie M will hear.'

'That's something else you're always going on about — Auntie M. The way you talk about her you'd think you were the only one who cared about her. Well, I care about her, too, Miss High and Mighty Laura Phelan. And what's more, I've already asked her if the music was too loud and she said she loves listening to it. So there,' Emma informed her and reaching out towards the ghettoblaster, turned the volume up even louder than before.

Later that evening, Laura decided to cycle over to 'Rosemount'.

The school classroom had been hot and stuffy and she felt like getting out into the fresh air. Besides she and Emma were still sniping at each other and at the moment the house wasn't big enough for the two of them.

'I'll open the windows and let in some air,' she informed her Mother, holding out her hand for the hall door key.

'Be sure to lock them securely before you leave, won't you.'

'Sure. Wouldn't want anyone to break in now that it's going to be put up for sale?' Laura said sarcastically.

Marjorie Phelan sighed as she watched her cycle off. Laura had changed so much this past while. Her daughter hardly talked to her any more, and when she did it seemed it was only to argue or pass some sarcastic remark as she'd done just now. The blonde woman bit her lip, her face looking more strained than usual. Where was it all going to end, she wondered. Maybe Laura would come round when Auntie M went into Milton House and she saw how well she was being looked after there. Maybe then she'd understand that what was being done was unavoidable and really for the best and would stop blaming her for the painful decision which had to be made. Well, at least for the next day or two there was something to look forward to — seeing her 'baby' brother, as she still thought of John. He'd phoned this afternoon to say he'd be paying a flying visit at the weekend. Even Auntie M had perked up at the prospect, although the reason for him coming wasn't the happiest. Oh Lord, there she was now, Marjorie Phelan thought, hearing the familiar 'thump, thump' on the ceiling. And, as had become her habit of late, she quickly mounted the stairs to see what it was her aunt wanted.

Laura decided to take the long way round and headed out along the coast road. As sometimes happened after a warm sunny day, she found that a heavy sea mist had fallen. She felt sorry for those people who had obviously driven straight out from work, hoping to have a pleasant hour or two by the sea before the sun went down. Quite a number of them were sitting in their cars, looking out disappointedly, while the braver ones had stepped out and now stood gazing out to sea as though expecting the mist to lift at any moment, like a huge stage curtain. Laura, born within walking distance of the seashore, knew they were not to get their wish, that the mist was down for the night. She could already feel the dampness in the air, but it was too late now to turn back and take the shorter route.

'Damn,' she thought, knowing that her hair, which she'd spent ages brushing out straight before she'd left, would soon begin to turn into a mass of wispy curls.

The mist had completely blotted out the view of Ireland's Eye. It was as if the small rocky island had never existed. As Laura looked out to where she knew it must be, she thought how marvellous it would be if the bad things in life could be blotted out as easily. If only some sort of curtain could be drawn, shutting them out as though they'd never happened. Had it been possible, she'd willingly have drawn such a curtain on the last few months, gladly have watched it close tightly on the scene that afternoon when she'd discovered her Great-aunt lying on the grass. But, of course, she knew it was silly and a waste of time thinking like that and so, concentrating on the road ahead, she began cycling furiously.

She hadn't been to the bungalow since her Great-aunt had taken ill and now as she slowed up and stopped outside the gate, she hesitated for a moment before pushing it open. Slowly she made her way up the path, thinking now of her Mother's words when she'd announced her intention of riding over.

'Are you sure, love? You haven't been there for a while. Maybe it'd be better to wait until your Father or I are going over?'

But, Laura had been adamant that she wanted to go alone. And now, here she was, not even sure if, after all, she had the courage to go inside. She wasn't afraid to be alone in the house. It wasn't anything like that. It was just that... just that on every other occasion she'd visited 'Rosemount,' Auntie M had been here, waiting for her, throwing the door open wide, a smile of greeting on her face. But there'd be no such greeting today, she knew, as biting back a sob, she turned the key in the hall door.

Something was different.

She could feel it the moment she stepped inside. A quick glance around the hall confirmed that everything was in its usual place. Yet something wasn't quite right — she was sure of it. She stood there in the silence, listening. And then she heard it — just the slightest sound. She waited, straining to hear it again. She did, and instantly she knew. She wasn't alone. There was someone else in the house...

A group of curious, excited class mates gathered round Laura in the school corridor, jostling each other to get her attention.

'Did they really lock you in a cupboard?'

'Did they hit you? Is that how you got the mark on your forehead?'

'What did they look like?'

'Did you recognise them?'

'Hey, give her a chance, will you,' Aishling said, pushing her way through to her friend's side. 'Can't you see she's still shaken. She shouldn't be in school at all.'

Aishling was right. Laura's Mother had wanted her to take the day off school after her ordeal of the night before, but she'd only managed to keep her at home for the morning. Laura had argued, and won, that she was fully recovered and was quite ready to go in after lunch break.

'Look, I'll start at the beginning. This is what happened,' Aishling said, taking over, quite enjoying the feeling of the dozens of attentive eyes which turned in her direction.

'Last night Laura went to check on her aunt's house, but when she got there...' Aishling paused making sure she still had her audience's undivided attention, 'she walked in on top of two guys robbing the place. They...'

'Gosh! What happened then,' someone from the back of the crowd wanted to know.

'If you'd stop interrupting, maybe I could manage to tell you,' Aishling snapped, waiting for silence before she continued.

'They obviously heard her open the hall door because as soon as she stepped inside...'

"As soon as I stepped inside," Laura wrote later, "a man wearing a balaclava burst out of the living room and came rushing towards me. He grabbed me. I was terrified and began to scream. Another man appeared then, saying 'For Jaysus sake, tie her up quick and put her in there or the whole neighbourhood will hear her.' Before I knew what was happening, I was gagged and my hands bound behind my back. Then they picked me up and carried me into the kitchen and pushed me into the broom cupboard, hanging my head against the door as they shut it. In the pitch black, I could hear them arguing outside.

'Thought ya said that hardly anyone came here,' the first man accused.

'Look. Haven't I been watchin' the joint for weeks. How the hell was I t'know that young one was goin' t'walk in on top of us?' the second man defended himself.

'OK. OK. Keep yer shirt on. Grab what ya can an' let's get outa here.'

I could hear them moving around noisily as they tried to find what they wanted. I prayed they wouldn't come near me again. The sensation I'd felt as they'd put their hands on me was something I didn't want to experience a second time. One of them did open the cupboard again before they finally left, but it was just to make sure I was tied up. 'No problem,' he called to his accomplice. 'She's scared outa her wits. This one won't cause us any trouble.' I almost cried with relief when he kicked the door shut and soon, mercifully, at last I heard them leave.

There was no use calling out — the gag was too tight — and I couldn't free my hands. The man had done a good job and the rope cut into my wrists each time I moved. I tried bringing my feet down hard against the door, but the burglars had obviously rammed something against it and it wouldn't budge an inch. I felt so helpless as I lay there in the dark. And angry too. Angry for allowing myself to be caught and angry with those men for daring to break into Auntie M's home.

I heard the phone ring several times and guessed it was either Mum or Dad wanting to know what was keeping me. Eventually, after ages, Dad arrived and found me. I can't describe how the place looked. Drawers had been pulled out everywhere, their contents emptied onto the floor. Bed covers had been pulled back and mattresses shifted. Pictures hung at peculiar angles and one or two — their glass smashed — had been walked into the floor. Even the medicine chest in the bathroom had been ransacked, with various bottles lying broken in the washhand basin. The place was a total mess. In the middle of all the debris, I came across a piece of crumpled brownish-coloured paper. I don't know what made me pick it up, but I did. When, out of curiosity, I smoothed it out as best I could, I realised it had to be the postcard Auntie M had bought for me weeks ago…

Of course, the Gardaí had to be called. They didn't exactly say, but I got the feeling that they didn't hold out much hope of catching the culprits! I hated it as I stood there watching even more strangers go through my Great-aunt's treasured possessions. And, of course, Mum made such a fuss when Dad and I finally arrived home. Not just about the bump on my forehead, and about putting in an alarm system. She kept going on and on about not telling Auntie M what had happened. As if I would! I know she's enough to cope with at the moment without telling her that her home has been ransacked! The worst part of it all is that now Mum's more convinced than ever that 'Rosemount' has to be sold. 'It'll be broken into again if it's left unoccupied much longer,' she told Dad at least half a dozen times. Wonder what Uncle John will think of all that's happening? Will he be against Milton House and selling the bungalow? I hope so. He's my only hope now."

CHAPTER SIX

The airport was swarming with people. Laura watched with interest as men, women and children of all nationalities passed through the arrivals section where she and her Mother waited. She'd decided to come with her to pick up her Uncle John from his flight. Her Mother had suggested it the night before, but Laura hadn't agreed to come simply to please her. She'd agreed because she was impatient to hear what her Uncle had to say about the plans being made for her Great-aunt's future, and her natural curiosity to see him after a gap of almost three years. They'd left her father at home, keeping an eye on Auntie M and, of course, Emma had decided to stay in bed, moaning that it was far too early an hour for her to get up on a Saturday morning. 'Suiting herself, as usual,' Laura had thought earlier, as she'd moved quietly about the bedroom so as not to waken her, knowing if she did it would only end in another row to add to all the others they'd had since they'd been made to share.

The announcement that flight EI 168 from London to Dublin had landed caused her Mother to look up from the newspaper she'd been reading. Folding it up she smiled at her daughter and said, 'Won't be long now.'

Laura didn't even bother to answer. Marjorie

Phelan's lips tightened into a thin line. It was impossible. No matter how hard she tried, she couldn't seem to get the relationship she'd once had with her daughter back onto its old footing. At times she really felt like giving up. She was beginning to get very tired of Laura's rude, moody behaviour and if it wasn't for her brother's imminent arrival, she'd have given her a piece of her mind right here and now. Biting back her anger, she kept her eyes glued to the arrivals gate.

'There he is,' she said a moment later, and half walking, half running made her way through the group of passengers towards a tall, brown haired man.

'Hi Sis,' he said, giving her a hug, and, smiling over her shoulder at his niece, 'You've certainly changed since last I saw you.'

Laura smiled shyly as they made their way to the conveyor belt to collect his case and then the three of them headed out to the car park.

'It's great to be home for a day or two,' her Uncle John said as he settled into the passenger seat beside her Mother, 'even if the reason for coming could be better, Sis.'

Laura knew he was referring to Auntie M, but, to her disappointment, it was the only reference he made about her during the drive home. He said nothing about the possibility of her going into the nursing home or the sale of 'Rosemount'. Her Mother and he seemed to find dozens of things to talk about, other than the topic which was uppermost in Laura's mind. Despite her disappointment, however, her uncle made her laugh several times during the journey and Laura found herself telling him about school, her friends and her hopes for the forthcoming badminton championships. She asked him all sorts of questions about her cousins, particularly his daughter Anna, who was the same age and for the first time in months, for a short while, her aunt and all the problems which were bothering her were pushed aside. Watching her in the rear view driving mirror, Marjorie Phelan smiled secretly as she caught a glimpse of the old Laura, relieved to see that she hadn't disappeared altogether.

Emma stepped right in front of her sister and studied herself in the long wardrobe mirror.

'How do I look?' she asked.

'Would it matter what I thought,' the older girl replied sarcastically.

'Not really,' Emma answered, equally sarcastically, before flouncing out of the room. Laura was left looking at her own reflection . She studied her new jeans. She liked the fit. Fit! The word took on a new meaning as she thought of the fit her Mother would have when she came downstairs wearing them. Uncle John had suggested that the whole family go out for a meal tonight.

'You could do with a break, Sis,' he'd insisted as they'd sat having a snack in the kitchen on their return from the airport. 'I don't like saying it, but I've seen you look a lot better.'

'Hey! Watch it,' Tom Phelan said to his brother-in-law 'Careful how you talk to my wife. She looks as beautiful as ever to me.'

His wife and brother-in-law laughed.

'Seriously though, John, I have to admit you're right,' he agreed. 'The strain of caring for Auntie M is telling on Marjorie but no matter what I do I can't get her to ease up and take a break Still, maybe she'll do it for you. How about it, love?' He turned to his wife. 'A night out would do the whole family good.'

With a little more persuasion from her brother and husband, Marjorie Phelan agreed, and so, after a quick telephone call to Sheelagh Dalton to see if she'd be willing to sit in and keep an eye on things, a table had been booked for 7.30 pm in the Winter Garden Restaurant.

'We'll need to be leaving at about seven o'clock. So be ready, you two.' Marjorie Phelan had warned her daughters, adding 'Oh, and wear something beside jeans, will you? Something suitable.'

Still looking at her reflection, for a moment Laura almost capitulated. She didn't enjoy going against her Mother like this, despite what she might think. But ever since she'd announced she could no longer keep on looking after Auntie M, and that she couldn't continue to live here with the family — that Milton House was the only answer — Laura had wanted to hurt her Mother in every way she could. Sometimes she was so filled with anger about the whole thing, that she wanted to punish herself as well. She could never completely manage to get out of her mind the fact that she'd been late that fateful afternoon.

'No,' she thought defiantly, turning away from the mirror. 'I'll wear them. I don't care how much it annoys her. Or how much she punishes me. It'll be worth it.'

Sheelagh Dalton and her Uncle John were standing in the hallway chatting when Laura finally came downstairs. Her Mother walked out of the living room to join them just as she reached the last step. She looked her daughter up and down, taking in the defiant toss of her blonde hair, the angry glint in her green eyes and, most of all, the jeans she wore. But she said nothing . Instead she turned to her brother indicating that it was time for them all to be on their way.

The food at the Winter Garden was always first class. Laura and her family had been there on several other occasions and had never had any cause for complaint. This evening it was up to its usual high standard, but by the time the party reached the dessert stage, Laura could hardly swallow another mouthful. Nobody noticed how tense she was. They were all too busy talking and laughing and enjoying their meal.

'And wait 'till I tell you about this...' It was her Uncle John again. He'd hardly stopped talking since they'd sat down. In the beginning she'd enjoyed listening to what he had to say, but as the evening progressed she couldn't believe it when not even once did he bring Auntie M's name into the conversation. Laura had hoped he'd try to persuade her Mother to at least wait another while, to see if there would be any improvement in her aunt's condition, before making any final decisions . He'd supposedly come all this way to help sort out arrangements about his aunt's future, yet so far Laura hadn't heard him mention a thing about it. As she sat listening to him go on and on about some stupid thing his youngest son had done, she wondered how he could behave like this. How could he continue making them laugh, not giving his aunt a second thought as she lay there at home, unable to move or speak properly. She'd tried to interrupt in the middle of one of his stories, but her Father had cut her short, saying 'Wait a sec. We just have to hear the end of this' and once again she'd had to endure the howls of laughter from all around the table. All at once she couldn't take any more of it. Uncle John was the same as the rest of them. He couldn't wait to wash his hands of the poor woman. Without even excusing herself, Laura stood up abruptly from the table and made her way to the ladies' toilet. On the verge of tears, and with her stomach in a knot, she felt suddenly sick. The meal she'd just eaten had left a taste like poison in her mouth.

"I stayed in bed as late as I could this morning. Emma was watching me as she dressed — giving me sly looks, wondering what was up. Just because I'm always up first! But she didn't say anything. Probably still cool with me for the way I answered her during her 'preening' session last night. Too bad!

Lunch, which I couldn't touch, was a repeat performance of dinner last night, with Uncle John telling even more of his ridiculous stories.

I spent the afternoon keeping Auntie M company. Uncle John came in and said a few things, but I couldn't be bothered talking. When Auntie M tried to say something to him, I knew by his face he couldn't understand a word. I felt so sorry for her, especially when he made a pretty quick exit.

I don't understand why he bothered to come at all!"

At the airport Marjorie Phelan kissed her brother goodbye.

'Sorry about Laura's behaviour, John. She's taking all this very badly. She's extremely attached to Auntie M, as you know. I think she was hoping that when you arrived you'd somehow manage to change things. Now, I'm afraid, she sees you as just another one of the "baddies".'

'I sort of got that feeling alright. She certainly gave me the cool treatment this afternoon. Couldn't get a word out of her. But look, Sis, don't worry. You'll see, when Auntie M is comfortably settled in the nursing home, Laura will come round again.'

'That's what I keep telling myself. Oh, I hope we're both right, John. I wish I could make her understand that none of us wanted this to happen, that life is never that simple.'

'Have you thought about changing your mind? About telling her, I mean.'

'You think I should?'

Laura's Uncle John nodded.

'Tom thinks the same thing, but I just can't John. Not yet anyway. Remember what happened last time? That's what I'm afraid of. And Laura has suffered enough upset and disappointments just now. I don't want her to be disappointed again...'

'I suppose you know best,' her brother said doubtfully, shaking his head sympathetically. 'Well, don't forget now, you take good care of yourself and if you've any trouble with a private sale, give me a buzz and I'll get in touch with my contact at Anderson & McCauley. He'll soon get things moving for you. They're said to be the best as far as estate agents are concerned.'

As she watched the tall, waving figure present his boarding card and disappear through security, Marjorie Phelan sighed. She knew that selling 'Rosemount' was something else she was going to have great difficulty in persuading her fractious daughter to accept.

CHAPTER SEVEN

By the following week the 'For Sale' advertisement had appeared in the national papers. On the same day, Laura's Mother phoned the Matron at Milton House and told her that her aunt would be taking up the vacancy and would be moving in at the end of the month. Although for weeks Laura had been bracing herself for all of this, now that it was actually happening she found she was still unprepared. And the speed with which things were moving left her almost stunned. She'd found it difficult to eat since the evening at the Winter Garden, and now this morning as she sat at the breakfast table she found it impossible.

'Aren't you going to eat any breakfast, Laura,' her mother asked looking at the untouched bowl of cereal on front of her daughter.

'I can't.'

'Why not? Are you sick or something?'

'No. I'm not sick.'

'Then why not?' There was a hint of exasperation in her Mother's tone.

'I just can't, I told you. I just can't.' Angrily Laura pushed the bowl away and getting up from the table, left the kitchen.

'What's wrong with her?' Emma asked, and, a moment later, as they heard the front door slam,

'Huh! Didn't even say goodbye!'

Her Mother shrugged, making no comment, relieved to see her quickly lose interest in her sister's sudden departure and return to her breakfast. With the way she felt right now, she knew that if Emma had said another word she'd have bitten her head off. It was bad enough being at loggerheads with Laura without having to feel guilty about venting her anger on an innocent party. She sighed. It had been like this since the day after John had gone back to London, from the time she'd told Laura that 'Rosemount' was definitely going to be sold. Every single morning since, she'd left the table, her breakfast untouched. But for the fact that the school had a canteen and she knew Laura could get a hot lunch each day, she'd have been worried sick about her. She probably stuffed herself silly then, she thought, because she didn't appear hungry when she came home in the evenings, not eating much at dinner time either.

'Bye, Mum.'

Emma's voice broke into her thoughts.

'Bye, love,' Marjorie Phelan said, kissing her younger daughter absentmindedly.

The hall door had only closed on Emma when she heard the sound of knocking from upstairs. Oh no, not her aunt awake already, she thought wearily, as the 'thump, thump' came again. She usually had time for a quiet cup of tea after the girls had left before taking up her breakfast, but it seemed as though the old lady was ready for it earlier than usual this morning. She heard the sound repeated yet again, but this time more urgently. Strange — her aunt wasn't usually impatient. And then, the thought suddenly flashed into her mind that perhaps it was more than breakfast she was calling for and filled with a sense of dread, she made a dash from the kitchen and headed up the stairs.

Mary Andrews was hanging out over the edge of the bed, her paralysed arm jammed between it and the bedside locker. Her knuckles showed white against her skin, as she clutched an old walking stick in her left hand. Feebly she raised it into the air and was about to bring it down hard,once again, on the bedroom floor when her niece burst into the room. She was so relieved to see Marjorie, that she immediately released her grip on it and let it fall uncaringly from her grasp.

'Oh! God,' her niece blurted, rushing to her.

With a pounding heart, she gently eased her Aunt's trapped arm free and settled her back carefully against the pillows.

'There now, Auntie M. You're all right,' she said as calmly as she could manage, trying to hide how upset she was. Her aunt mumbled something but, as usual when she was agitated, it was difficult to make out what it was.

'You were trying to reach for a hankie, was that it?'

The old lady nodded, tears filling her eyes.

'There, there, Auntie M. There's no need to be upset, you're alright now. I'll move the box of tissues nearer. You just relax and I'll go and get you some breakfast,' Laura's mother said, patting her gently on the shoulder.

Outside on the landing, her composure began to slip. A wave of nausea swept over her and her whole body started to tremble. Only yesterday there'd been a similar upsetting incident. She'd managed to get her aunt from the bed to an armchair beside the window, where she could see out, when the phone had started to ring. She'd been expecting John to call and, thinking perhaps it was long distance, had quickly settled her aunt in the chair before hurrying to see who it was. After only a few brief words with Mrs O'Sullivan, her aunt's old neighbour, who'd recently taken to ringing as well as visiting, she'd returned to the room to find her charge bent over, holding her forehead. Mary Andrews had somehow misjudged the height of the window sill and had leaned forward in the chair hitting her head against it. Marjorie had been frightened that she'd reopened the cut she'd suffered during her stroke, but was relieved to see that it looked alright. Just above it, however, was a bright red mark, which this morning had turned a bluish colour and was slightly swollen.

Poor Auntie M. She'd always been so good to her and John, yet she couldn't take much more of this. From now on she knew that every time she heard that knocking she'd be fearful of what it meant. What if she'd been out of the house, even for a short while, when this happened? Her Aunt could have been lying over the edge of the bed, unable to pull herself upright, until she'd returned. She hardly ever left her alone these days, but there were times when she simply had to go out. Although after what had just happened, she knew that from this until Auntie M moved to Milton House these occasions would be rarer than ever. Pity Laura hadn't been here just now, she thought as she headed downstairs into the kitchen. Maybe it would have made her realise just how much her aunt needed round the clock care and attention. Care which she could no longer continue to give, especially now that... But for the moment she pushed the matter to the back of her mind and instead, popping some bread into the toaster, set about preparing her aunt's breakfast.

Lying back limply against the pillows listening to her niece moving around downstairs, Mary Andrews was thinking exactly the same thing. The present situation couldn't continue. Although her limbs would no longer behave as she wished them to, and she almost always failed to make herself understood, her thoughts weren't in the least bit muddled. She could see her niece was exhausted with all she had to do and she knew her presence in the house was causing friction between members of the family. She wasn't blind to the looks Laura gave her Mother, nor was she deaf to her insolent answers. She could see, too, that Emma hated sharing a bedroom, and the walls weren't thick enough to prevent her hearing the regular arguments between the two girls. She felt she was a burden on all of them, but especially on Marjorie. She'd been thinking about the future a lot these past weeks. She knew she'd never be well enough again to take care of herself, to be able to return to her own home. But she'd been reluctant to suggest moving into a nursing home in case she might hurt Marjorie, perhaps make her feel she was unhappy here with her and her family. She'd been relieved when the subject had finally come up during one of their rather disjointed conversations. She wasn't really sure now which of them had first broached the idea of a nursing home, but it had made it so much easier for both of them to find they'd been thinking along the same lines. But Marjorie, bless her, she thought fondly, had refused to make a final decision until John had paid them a visit. Thank God he'd agreed, Mary Andrews thought as she wiped away a tear. Her moving into Milton House would be the best thing for all of them. Although the family showered her with love and attention, she knew she couldn't remain here and expect them to look after her indefinitely. If she stayed, eventually they were bound to resent the burden she'd become, and that was the last thing she wanted. No, the nursing home was the only option. She'd get the professional care and attention which she needed there. And hold on to whatever little independence she had left.

Not that Laura saw it that way. Poor Laura, she was so confused about everything. If only she could manage to explain things to her. But she found it so difficult since her stroke to make herself understood, to get the words to come out clearly. Marjorie seemed to be the only one who had any idea of what she was trying to say. And she couldn't write down what she was thinking either — her damn left hand would insist on rambling all over the page! Even if she did manage something, she had a strong feeling the girl wouldn't believe her. She seemed determined to blame her Mother for everything just now.

With the help of the pulley, she shifted her body

slightly in the bed. She cursed her helplessness and all the problems it was causing. God, how she hated being confined to this bed for long hours on end. Turning her face into her pillow, Mary Andrews wept.

CHAPTER EIGHT

'Well, even though I say it myself, you were BRILLIANT!' Deirdre O'Brien laughed as she looked at the flushed, excited faces of her players. Both the 'A' and 'B' teams were now through to the finals. She'd been a bit worried about Laura Phelan, who'd been looking pretty tired and pale when the match had begun, but, to her relief, in the end the girl had played extraordinarily well.

Over all the excited chatter, it was difficult to make herself heard. Clapping her hands together to get their attention, she called out 'Hurry and change now and when you're ready come on upstairs. The home team has laid on a fabulous spread.'

'Feeling OK?' Aishling asked, turning to her friend. Like Deirdre O'Brien she'd noticed how pale and drawn Laura had looked earlier.

'Yeah, fine. Just had a few cramps in my stomach at the beginning of play.'

'Nerves maybe?'

'Maybe.'

Satisfied that Laura was all right, Aishling turned aside to talk to one of the players from the team they'd beaten. For the moment Laura was left with her own thoughts. She'd lied to Aishling just now. It hadn't been nerves which had caused her to have cramps. Every time she thought of the newspaper cutting buried at the bottom of her sports bag she got a knot in her stomach. She'd cut it out of the morning paper and had shoved it in beneath all her gear just before she'd left the house. Now as she sat there, not making any real effort to get changed, she found herself silently repeating over and over what it said.

'Nearly ready?' a voice asked, startling her.

Laura looked up blankly. It was one of the girls from the home team.

'Ready to come upstairs for something to eat?' she asked pleasantly, indicating in the direction of Aishling and the other girls who were now changed and ready to go. Laura shook her head.

'Sorry, 'fraid not just yet. But you lot go on ahead. I'll follow as soon as I can.'

'I wouldn't take too long if I were you,' the girl advised smilingly, 'otherwise all the best goodies will be gone.'

'I won't,' Laura said, forcing a smile as she watched her go over to join the others.

The minute the chattering group had left the changing room, she began rummaging through her things until she found the scrap of paper. Although she knew every word of it off by heart, Laura began reading it yet again .

For Sale spacious 3 bed bungalow.
Large Sit/Din room, good sized kitchen, oil fired central heating, situated approx. 1/4 acre, mature garden...

No matter how often she read it, Laura couldn't see anything in those cold, black, printed words which painted a picture of the 'Rosemount' she knew. They didn't describe the warm welcoming house where she'd spent so many happy afternoons and weekends. 'Mature garden' told nothing of the loving care lavished by her Great-aunt on the numerous plants and shrubs, gave no hint of the wonderful display of colour when all the rose bushes were in full bloom. Especially those on the slightly raised area at the back of the bungalow from which 'Rosemount' had derived its name. They gave no hint, either, of how even in the dead of winter the garden still showed signs of life where Auntie M had planted several winter cherryblossoms.

'I'm going to do everything I can to stop them selling it,' she'd whispered, showing the cutting to Aishling as they'd sat in the back of the minibus on their way to this afternoon's match.

'But how, Laura?'

'I don't know yet, but you can bet on it — I'll think of something.

Listening to her friend speak with such certainty, Aishling was convinced she would.

As soon as she got home Laura made straight for her Great-aunt's room to tell her of the team's success. Her mother called from the kitchen as she was going up the stairs.

'How'd it go, Laura?'

'We're through,' she answered without stopping.

It was all so unfair she thought as she reached the landing. If only Auntie M was her old self, if only she was friends with her Mother as she'd always been, today's win would have meant so much more to her.

Under normal circumstances she'd have rushed into the kitchen to share the excitement of winning with her, the thrill of getting through to the finals. But nothing was the same anymore.

Auntie M smiled slightly distractedly as she listened to her relate all that had happened.

'It was pretty close at one stage…'

Laura stopped, becoming aware of what her aunt had been doing when she came into the room. She had a dark blue velvet box on the bed beside her and she appeared to be sorting through it with what she called her 'good' arm, while her right one hung uselessly by her. Seeing her niece's eyes on the box, the old lady began fumbling awkwardly through the contents. Laura was overwhelmed with pity as she watched, seeing how difficult the simple task was. Raising her head unexpectedly, Mary Andrews met her gaze. Immediately Laura conjured up a smile.

'What're you doing?' she asked in an attempt to divert her Great-aunt's attention as she blinked back tears which she knew must be all too visible.

'Sorting…few…fings. Can't take eve…ry…fing to…. 'ursing home.'

To Laura's relief, she understood her aunt's reply. She hated having to ask her to repeat things, or to witness her having to sort through her word cards until she found one which helped make clearer what she was trying to say.

Now her aunt pointed to the box.

'What is it? Do you want me to get you something out of it?'

'Choo… cho…ose sum…fing for 'sef'. Her aunt spoke again, but not so clearly this time.

'You mean something to keep, Auntie M.'

'Course, 'course,' the reply was sharp and impatient.

Laura leaned forward and studied the contents of the box. She knew exactly what she was looking for. It was something she'd always admired when her Great-aunt had worn it. She'd bought it on one of their Sunday afternoon jaunts — a filigree broach in the shape of a butterfly. Lifting up a string of pearls, she found it hidden beneath. Carefully she took it out and placed it in the palm of her hand. It was so delicate, she thought as she looked down at it and then, smiling up at her aunt, she said softly 'This.... this is what I'd like. But are you sure you want to part with it?'

Her aunt nodded in confirmation and Laura leaned forward and gave her a kiss on the cheek. The thought of Auntie M not being here in just a very short while was all too much for her and, for once, she was glad to hear Emma come pounding up the stairs and seconds later see her burst into the room.

'Oh, that's gorgeous. Where'd you get it?' she asked, seeing the broach in Laura's hand.

'Auntie M.'

'Got anything for me?,' Emma asked cheekily, turning to their aunt, who was already shakily holding out the contents of the blue velvet box to the younger girl.

Laura got up and quietly left the room, Emma's chatter following her. It was well for Emma, she thought, as she went into their bedroom. She didn't seem to be at all bothered by what was happening. As far as she was concerned Auntie M was just going somewhere else to live. She didn't seem to realise the enormity of it all, didn't seem to realise that she would spend the remainder of her life at Milton House and she would never, ever go back to her own home again. Someday somebody was going to burst that bubble her sister lived in. There were times she was so insensitive that Laura felt like throttling her and, as she looked around the bedroom and saw that it was in an even worse mess than usual, she felt like doing it right now.

After rummaging through almost every single item of jewellry belonging to her Great-aunt, Emma finally settled on a pair of drop earrings. They were, of course, far too grown up for her, but Mary Andrews hadn't the heart to point out that fact and simply smiled in agreement as the young girl went out the bedroom door happy with her choice. Emma — so different to Laura, her Great-aunt thought. She knew Laura had been upset when she'd left the room earlier, while just now her sister had floated off without a care in the world!

She glanced into the mirror on the inside lid of the blue velvet box. Her image looked back at her and she put a hand to her bare neck. It struck her that it had been an age since she'd worn any of her jewellry, but then, she thought with a wry smile, bed wasn't exactly the place to have oneself dripping with necklaces and bracelets! Still, it mightn't be a bad idea to put on just a pair of earrings, she decided, clipping a small pearl onto her left earlobe The right one proved to be a little more difficult, but, after a bit of a struggle, she finally managed it. There, she thought, looking once again at her reflection, that was much better. When the family saw her sporting those, maybe they'd believe her spirits weren't quite as low as they'd thought. It certainly wouldn't do any harm if wearing them helped to cheer Marjorie up a little. She'd noticed that she seemed extra quiet of late. Mary Andrews was only too aware of how short a time was left now before she was due to move to Milton House and, as far as she was concerned, she was determined to do everything in her power to make her leaving as easy as possible for all concerned.

Sheelagh Dalton was taken by surprise with her daughter's question. They'd been discussing that afternoon's badminton match when, tired but happy after her win, Aishling had unexpectedly changed the subject and asked 'What's all the rush about putting Mrs Andrews into a home, Mum?'

'Rush? Who says there's a rush?'

'Well, Laura for one. She says her Mother can't wait to get her out of the house.'

'Hmmm...Does she now? I don't think that's quite true.'

'She seems to think so. Her aunt's house is up for sale, too. Did you know that?'

'Yes. Marjorie mentioned it one morning when we had coffee together.'

'Did she say anything else?'

'What about?' Sheelagh Dalton sounded suspicious.

'Well...just things.'

'You mean about Mrs Andrews and the nursing

home?'

Aishling's face reddened slightly.

'Is it you or Laura who wants to know?' her Mother asked.

When her daughter didn't answer, Sheelagh Dalton went on 'Look. I know your friend is upset about what's happening, but I also know that her Mother wouldn't let her aunt go to a nursing home if there was any way she could avoid it. I know…eh…I mean I'm sure she's a very good reason for doing it.'

Quick as lightening Aishling asked 'What reason?'

'I don't know.'

'But you said…'

'Aishling. Marjorie Phelan knows what's best for Mrs Andrews. All I can say is that I'm very grateful I'm not faced with a similar decision about one or other of your grandparents. Now I've nothing more to say on the subject,' Aishling's Mother said firmly, silently admitting that she'd already said far too much about things as it was.

CHAPTER NINE

Tom Phelan sat in the car waiting for his wife to join him. Tonight was his and Marjorie's bridge night and, having cried off for the past few weeks complaining of feeling tired, Marjorie had surprised him this evening when he'd arrived home by saying she was looking forward to coming along to tonight's session. Glancing at his watch, he saw they were cutting it fine if they wanted to be on time and he gave the car horn a gentle tap. Inside the house Laura's mother pulled on her coat and, turning to her daughter said 'We won't be late. If there are any calls about the ad for the house, take the phone numbers and say I'l ring them in the morning, will you, Laura?' Sullenly Laura agreed.

As soon as the hall door closed on her Mother, Laura went into the living room and turned up the television to drown out the noise of Emma's 'music' coming from the room overhead. She flicked from one channel to the next, but found nothing of interest. Restless and looking for something to occupy her, she decided to do a bit of extra study to pass the time. Going upstairs she braved the deafening onslaught of heavy metal from her sister's ghettoblaster, quickly grabbed her schoolbooks from the shelf above her bed and got out of the room as fast as she could. On the way down, she looked in on her Great-aunt to make sure she was alright and, to her amazement discovered that, despite the racket, she was sleeping soundly.

Downstairs again, Laura found she couldn't settle down to study either. She was praying that the phone wouldn't ring, yet she couldn't relax knowing that the chances were it would. It hadn't stopped the night before, but to her relief, and her Mother's disappointment, for one reason or another none of the calls had come to anything. 'Rosemount' had proved too expensive for some people, or too far from the city centre for others. If only there was some way she could prevent it from being sold, she thought for what must have been the thousandth time! She sat there thinking about it, racking her brain in an effort to come up with something. There had to be a way, she told herself over and over until eventually, bit by bit, an idea began to take shape in her mind.

When the phone did ring, Laura jumped.

Lifting the receiver she found it was Aishling on the other end of the line.

'Oh! Hi there, Aishling.' There was a a mixture of disappointment and relief in her voice.

'You sound different. What's the matter?' her friend asked.

'Different? Do I? Yeah, suppose I do. Listen, Aishling. I can't go into details now, but I've come up with something.'

'You mean about "you know what"?' Aishling was equally mysterious.

'Right first time.'

'Me, too.'

'What!'

'Yes. I brought up "the subject" with my Mother this evening…'

'And,' Laura interrupted, hardly able to contain herself.

'Well, nothing concrete. But I've a feeling she knows something. She got quite flustered when I kept on probing.'

'Gosh!'

'Better not talk over the phone. I'll tell you all tomorrow. OK?'

'OK Aishling.'

'See you then, Laura.'

'See you. Bye.'

'Who was that?' Emma's voice asked from the top of the stairs.

'Aishling,' Laura told her, trying to keep the irritation out of her voice, surprised that her sister had managed to hear the phone ring with the terrible noise that was still going on. Satisfied, Emma went back into their room, closing the door behind her. Why couldn't she have gone over to her friend, Blainid, for a while, Laura quietly fumed, cursing her sister's presence in the house at this particular time. She'd never be able to carry out what she planned if Emma kept popping in and out every time the phone went. She decided not to take any chances and from then on stood beside it, ready to lift the receiver the minute it rang.

"I did it! I did it! I told everyone who phoned that 'Rosemount' was already sold! The first time was hardest. My mouth went completely dry and when I started to speak I made the most terrible croaking sound. Most of them accepted what I said right away, although there was one man who asked a few awkward questions! But I managed to get rid of him eventually. I was terrified Emma would appear out of her room in the middle of it all, but luckily she didn't. I checked on Auntie M, too, in between each call and thankfully found her asleep every time.

When Mum got back I could see she was disappointed when I told her there hadn't been "a peep out of the phone all night". Except, of course, for Aishling. Which reminds me, I wonder what she has to tell me, what she meant by her Mother getting flustered. Can't wait to meet up with her tomorrow."

'Huh! A very good reason! I'm sure she has,' Laura said scornfully as she walked along beside her friend on their way to school next morning.

'Well, I'm only telling you what my Mother said.' Aishling's tone was hurt.

'OK. OK. Sorry. But as far as I can see the only reason she has for wanting Auntie M out of the house is that it's too much bother to take care of her.'

'Does your Dad ever say anything about what's happening?'

'Dad? No, he doesn't say anything, but I've noticed he's acting differently. Mum had to spend a few days in bed a while ago. She was complaining of a tummy bug, but she didn't look all that bad to me. What surprised me was that Dad actually took time off work to look after her, so that she could stay in bed. He's never done anything like that before. He's been fussing about her ever since, asking if she's tired, saying it won't be long now until things are sorted out. I mean, she doesn't have to do everything. I help all I can.' Tears of anger sprang to Laura's eyes as she spoke.

The two girls were quiet for a moment and then Aishling asked, 'By the way, you sounded very mysterious when I rang last night. What was it you wanted to tell me?'

Laura's expression brightened somewhat at her friend's question.

'I'll tell you, but I bet you won't believe it.'

'Try me,' Aishling encouraged.

'OK then, listen…'

When Laura had finished filling her in about the phone calls of the night before Aishling stared at her, dumbfounded.

'Gosh, Laura, I'd never have the nerve to do anything like that.'

'Yes you would — if you had to.' Laura was serious as she spoke. 'It was the last thing I'd have thought I'd ever do, but I had to, Aishling. I simply had to.'

'You'll be in big trouble if they find out.'

'How could they. No one heard, and those people aren't likely to call back again.'

'Well, for your sake, I hope they don't.'

'I heard Mum talking to Dad afterwards…' Laura paused for maximum effect, 'and she said that if 'Rosemount' isn't sold quickly it will be impossible to keep Auntie M in Milton House for any length of time!' Her face wore a triumphant look as she finished.

'Well, I can understand that,' Aishling said. 'Who could afford to pay...what did you say it was, Laura, over two hundred pounds a week?'

'That's right. Two hundred and sixty to be exact. Do you know something, Aishling? I'm beginning to believe that things may actually work out yet.'

But Laura's hopes were destined to be short lived. Unknown to her, further plans for the sale of her aunt's property were very soon to be put in motion.

The following afternoon when she arrived home from school she found her Mother on the phone. Walking past where she stood in the hall, she went into the kitchen, leaving the door open just enough so as to be able to hear what was being said.

'You think you should be able to contact your friend in the estate agents before lunchtime tomorrow, then, John?'

So, it was her Uncle in London her Mother was speaking to. And the mention of estate agents left her in no doubt as to what it was they were discussing.

'Yes, I've made a note of the name — Anderson & McCauley,' her Mother went on. 'I agree — going to an estate agent is probably better, although Tom and I did think something might have materialised as a result of the newspaper advertisement. Anyway, the sooner we get things moving again the better.'

It seemed then that her performance last night hadn't done any good at all, Laura thought dismally as she listened. It seemed, too, that an advertisement in the paper wasn't the only way to go about selling. She'd been stupid to think things could have worked out so easily, she realised now. She'd seen the situation as simply a case of no sale, no money, no nursing home! But now things were being taken a step further and there was nothing she could do to prevent it. It was only a matter of time before some stranger moved into her aunt's lovely home, and next Sunday, which was less than a week away now, Auntie M herself would move out of here and into that other, awful place.

CHAPTER TEN

"Today was the worst day of my life.

Up till now I'd always thought the afternoon I found Auntie M lying unconscious on the grass was the worst day I'd ever experienced, but at least then I could do something — keep her warm, ring for help, stay with her till the ambulance arrived. But today I could do nothing except watch as they wheeled her out to the car.

I said goodbye to her upstairs in her room. She asked me to come to see her often. I'll never forget the expression on her face when I didn't say I would. But I couldn't. I just couldn't make a promise I knew I wouldn't keep. I can't ever see myself going to visit her in that place.

I could have screamed at Emma. She was almost dancing around with excitement. You'd think she was off on some Sunday afternoon jaunt. The stupid girl doesn't seem to have a clue how heartbreaking this must all be for Auntie M! When Dad was folding up the wheelchair to put it into the boot, Mum whispered something to him and then came back and asked me again if I wouldn't change my mind and go with them.

'Laura,' she said, giving me her usual teary-eyed look, 'won't you change your mind and come with us?'

I shook my head.

'Please Laura,' she begged, 'I know how you must feel.'

'Know how I feel?' I almost shouted. 'No you don't. No one knows how I feel, no one knows how much I love Auntie M.'

'But we all love her, Laura,' she had the nerve to say.

'Well, if loving her means putting her into that Milton House, then you've a funny way of showing it,' I told her. 'And what's more, I'll never go to see her there. Never, never, never...."

After they'd gone, Laura lay on her bed for a long time, crying. When she finally stopped, she got up, bathed her swollen eyes and then went and sat on front of her dressing table mirror and idly began to brush her hair. The afternoon stretched depressingly before her. She knew her family wouldn't be back for at least a few hours, but that didn't bother her. Right now she felt she hated all three of them and was in no mood for their company. But it would have been nice to have someone to talk to. Aishling was the only one who understood how she was feeling these days. But even she wasn't around today. This weekend, Laura thought enviously, the lucky girl was enjoying herself with her family in Wexford.

Putting down her hair brush, she lifted the lid from the jewellry box on the dressing table in front of her and took out the little filigree butterfly. Gently she traced the outline of it with her finger. As she did so, she became aware of how deathly quiet it was and, for a moment, found herself listening — almost half expecting to hear the thump of her Great-aunt's walking stick coming from the room next door. As though she had to convince herself that the old lady was really gone, Laura got up and went and stood in the doorway of the other room.

'It'll be Emma's again tomorrow,' she thought sadly as she looked at the now empty bed and, feeling her tears start up again, turned quickly away.

'I'll go out somewhere,' she said aloud, the sound of her voice only serving to emphasise just how quiet the house was.

Within minutes she was outside and walking down the road, but with no particular destination in mind. She glanced about hoping that maybe she'd bump into someone from school. Anyone would do, just so long as they took her mind off things. But, as usual, on Sunday afternoon the road seemed particularly quiet with hardly a car in any of the driveways. It was as though the whole neighbourhood, except for her, had gone off somewhere for the afternoon. Seeing a bus turn the corner, she raced to the nearest stop and held up her hand for it to pull in.

'City centre.' she said jumping on and, handing over her fare, climbed to the upper deck. Here she found herself alone again, with not one other single passenger occupying the upstairs section. There was nothing to distract her, not even the back of someone's head and, as the vehicle trundled along, she found herself thinking of other Sunday afternoons. Afternoons so different to this. Afternoons when the sun had shone and the family had driven out into the country. Sunday afternoons when there'd been no sunshine, when it had even rained and they'd still headed off, content to sit and eat their sandwiches in the car . It hadn't really seemed to matter, they'd all been so happy then — her Mother and Father, she and Emma, and, of course, Auntie M.

By the time the bus turned into Lower Abbey Street, Laura had decided she'd go the cinema. She made her way round to Marlborough Street and turned up the side of the Pro-Cathedral. She quickly averted her eyes when, halfway down Cathedral Street, she drew level with a small shop window which displayed a variety of old coins and scores of medals from, now almost forgotten, wars. They only served to remind her of yet other treasured Sunday afternoons spent browsing around the antique stalls with her Great-aunt. With a toss of her head, briskly she headed into O'Connell Street.

There was a long queue outside the Savoy, but she joined it anyway. She saw that Jurassic Park was showing, and, although not particularly interested in dinosaurs, decided it couldn't be any worse than walking the streets aimlessly and, anyway, she might as well see what all the hype was about. The queue moved slowly and it was almost twenty minutes before she finally found herself at the ticket desk. She didn't bother to go to the sweet counter to treat herself. Nowadays she found she had hardly any interest in food. Instead, she headed straight for the auditorium, handing up her ticket to the usherette at the entrance.

The film was noisey, as might be expected, with one roaring dinosaur after another filling the large screen. But she found it much less frightening than she'd been led to expect. As she left the cinema, she could see from the faces of some of the children around her that they'd obviously enjoyed the whole thing, although for her, Laura had to admit, it had only been a means to while away the time. And it had, too, she thought gratefully, as she saw from her watch that it was almost seven o'clock.

'They'll be home by now,' she thought, but couldn't bring herself to go for the bus just yet. The thought of having to listen to her Mother quote the Matron, yet again, that Auntie M would 'settle in beautifully,' was more than she'd be able to take. She began walking slowly on down O'Connell Street, anxious to put off, if only for a short while the decision to go home. When she reached the end of the street, she crossed over onto the bridge where she stood for a minute or two looking over the parapet. She stared down into the Liffey as it flowed sluggishly beneath. Its murky waters seemed to reflect her own dark mood. After a minute or two, she crossed the wide thoroughfare, and began walking aimlessly up the other side, wondering what she could do to fill in another hour or two. As she passed one brassy fast-food outlet after another, Laura couldn't help but think that the once beautiful street left a lot to be desired. The smell of hot dogs and hamburgers drifted out from each as she walked by. But she wasn't tempted, not feeling in the least bit hungry. She did feel, however, that she'd like something to drink and seeing the familiar red and yellow sign of McDonald's a little further up headed towards it. She spent as long as she could sipping her coke, until, as the place started to fill up with more people than there was actually room for, she began to feel embarrassed about taking up a seat for so long, and got up and left.

Clery's clock told her it was half past eight.

She lingered in front of the shop window, still loath to go home. She lost track of how long she stood there, but, in the end, by the time she turned away and, reluctantly, set off in the direction of her bus, Laura must have known the price of every single item which had been on display.

Laura could make out the tall, well-built figure of her Father silhouetted against the hall light as he stood in the porch. She'd nearly died of shock when, hopping off the bus, she'd realised that it was going for a quarter to eleven. She was in big trouble and she knew it! She began to hurry, even though she was aware it was a bit late for that now. Tom Phelan said nothing as his daughter turned in the gate, and still remained silent when she stepped into the porch. It was only after the hall door had been closed behind her that he asked.

'Where in God's name have you been?' He managed to keep his voice surprisingly low for a man who, his frightened daughter could tell, was burning with anger. Before Laura could even answer he went on 'Do you realise the state your Mother is in? We've been ringing around hospitals since nine o'clock thinking you'd been involved in some sort of accident.'

'I...I went into town. I just thought...'

Her Father raised his hand in the air and for a moment Laura thought he was going to strike her. But to her relief, in a somewhat despairing gesture, he dropped it to his side, saying harshly

'You just thought. You just thought. You didn't think at all, that's the problem. You've thought of no one but yourself these past weeks. You've thought of nothing but how you feel about everything. How do you think your Mother feels? How do you think I feel? And, how the hell do you think your aunt felt today with you refusing even to accompany her to the nursing home?'

'But Daddy...'Laura said, beginning to cry.

'It's no good crying now. The damage has been done. You've upset the whole house, not even leaving a note to say where you'd gone. Go up to your room immediately and don't disturb your Mother. I've made her go to bed. She's exhausted.'

Only too glad to escape, Laura raced up the stairs. She didn't dare switch on the light in the bedroom, even though she knew Emma was awake by the huge, faked sigh the younger girl gave as she came into the room. All she wanted was to get into bed, close her eyes and try to shut out all that had happened. Swiftly pulling off only her outside garments, she slipped in and huddled down beneath the covers.

She slept fitfully, the dark hours of slumber filled with nightmarish dreams. Once she found herself being pursued by huge, roaring creatures. But when they finally cornered her in what appeared to be a small cave, she saw that they were, in fact, men wearing balaclavas who resembled, in a strangely grotesque way, the men she'd been confronted with during the robbery at her Great-aunt's house. One of them raised a hand to strike her, pulling off his mask with the other, and as she cowered beneath him she saw that it was her Father's angry face that glared down at her. She woke in fright, confused as to where she was, until, greatly relieved, she heard Emma's steady breathing coming from the bed opposite.

"Dad had already left for work, so at least I didn't have to face him. I managed to ignore Emma, although she was sitting there at breakfast smirking all over her face. At one stage she'd the nerve to ask me if I'd slept well!

Mum spent most of the time standing by the stove, her back to me. I know I should have apologised for yesterday, that I should have asked how Auntie M was when they left her. But I couldn't bring myself to do it. I just can't forgive Mum for what she's done. What really did surprise me though was that she wasn't even angry with me. She didn't even get at me for not eating as she usually does! I'm just about to leave for school now and she hasn't spoken to me at all!"

After the girls had gone, Marjorie Phelan poured herself a cup of tea and, leaning against the kitchen worktop, gazed unseeingly out into the back garden.

Her thoughts were a jumble of all that had happened in the last day or two. This was the first time in months she'd had the house to herself and, as she raised the cup to her lips, she paused for a moment, and, just as her daughter had done the afternoon before, waited, half expecting to hear her aunt's familiar signal from above. Poor Auntie M. She hoped she wasn't too unhappy. But it was Laura now she was really worried about. Things had never been so strained between them before. They'd always been close, not just as Mother and daughter, but good friends, too. She'd wanted to talk to her this morning, to at last break the news to her, to leave her in no doubt as to why she'd had to make the heartbreaking decision about her aunt. But at the moment she was so angry with Laura for her behaviour yesterday that she doubted she'd have found the right words. In the end, she'd decided the best thing to do was to say nothing at all for the moment. But had it really been the best, she wondered, as she drained her cup and rinsed it under the tap? She didn't really know.

Tom Phelan braked sharply.

He gave a low whistle as the car came to an abrupt stop only inches from the rear bumper of the vehicle in front.

'Phew, that was close,' he admitted silently. 'Damn traffic always stopping and starting.'

But the truth was he hadn't been concentrating, his mind hadn't been on the road at all. He'd been miles away.

Laura! What a problem she'd become, he thought

as he sat there, waiting impatiently for the long stream of traffic ahead to start moving. He knew that the last months had been difficult for her. They'd been difficult for all of them, but her behaviour yesterday had been the last straw. If his wife hadn't practically begged him to go easy on her, he'd have let her see just how angry he was. But he hadn't wanted to go against Marjorie, particularly at the moment. Yesterday had been traumatic enough for her without having to witness him telling Laura exactly what he thought of what she'd done. Arriving back from Milton House and finding their daughter wasn't at home had been bad enough, but as the evening wore on and there'd still been no sign of her they'd become frantic with worry. After ringing around all the local hospitals and finding out that, thankfully, she hadn't been involved in any kind of accident, for one terrible moment they'd even thought she might have run away. Tom Phelan had been on the verge of calling the police when he'd finally seen Laura walking up the road towards the house.

What was it with Laura all of a sudden, he wondered? He knew she'd taken it badly about her Great-aunt, much worse than they'd ever anticipated, but enough was enough. Sometimes he wondered if coming in upon those men that night at 'Rosemount' had had more of an effect on her than she let on. But, whenever he asked her about it, or tried to find out if it was playing on her mind, his daughter put up a barrier and told him adamantly 'I'm all right, Dad, don't fuss. I never even think about it.'

Maybe if, right from the start, they'd told the girls

the real reason for their aunt having to go into the nursing home things would have been different. But Marjorie hadn't been ready and, it seemed, still wasn't.

Well, he'd managed to keep his temper reasonably under control when Laura had come home last night, but he wasn't so sure he'd have managed to exercise the same amount of control at breakfast this morning. Especially after seeing the restless night Marjorie had spent, now when she needed her rest more than ever! So, he'd decided to leave early and avoid coming face to face with his daughter. Early! Fat lot of good it had done him traffic-wise, he fumed as he pushed his glasses up further onto the bridge of his nose. With a sigh he inched the car forward slightly, but the traffic ahead still remained stationary. Half the population of Dublin seemed to be making a determined effort to converge on the city centre, Tom Phelan thought, as he prepared to sit there even longer. Switching on the radio, he tried to relax as the familiar voice of *Morning Ireland*'s David Hanley came over the airwaves.

Laura's parents weren't the only ones concerned about her.

Aishling Dalton was worried too. It was more than a week now since Mrs Andrews had gone into the nursing home. Aishling thought that by now Laura would, at least, have begun to accept the idea, but instead she was more quiet and withdrawn than ever and when she did talk it was always about 'Rosemount'. Quite a few people appeared to be interested in it, and Laura had told her that the estate agents were arranging for two more couples to view it tomorrow night. She knew that her friend was still hoping against hope that her parents wouldn't find a buyer, but, somehow, Aishling had the feeling that within the next couple of weeks Laura's hopes would, once and for all, be dashed.

They'd been queueing patiently in the school canteen, and now when they'd at last reached the service hatch, Aishling couldn't believe it when she heard Laura ask only for a can of orange.

'Orange! Is that all you're going to have?' she said, looking down at her own plate, overflowing with sausage and chips and one of her favourite doughnuts.

'I don't feel like anything today,' Laura told her by way of explanation.

'You said that the other day, too.'

'Oh shut up, will you Aishling. It's bad enough my Mother trying to stuff breakfast into me every morning, without you starting on me too,' Laura retorted angrily.

Aishling watched as she turned away and headed over to a table at the far side of the canteen. She was really worried about her friend. The other day at badminton practice when they were all changing into their skirts and tops, she'd been surprised to see that Laura had lost quite a bit of weight. In fact, thought Aishling, Laura had not been herself since her Auntie M had become sick. She also hoped that these changes were not going to affect Laura's concentration on their sport. The finals were coming up pretty soon and they'd all need to be as fit as possible to give them the best chance of winning. Ordering

another doughnut, Aishling worked her way through
the tables towards where Laura was sitting, hoping
that, with a little gentle persuasion, she might be able
to tempt her yet.

CHAPTER ELEVEN

Laura couldn't believe it.

She'd known all along that 'Rosemount' should never have been put up for sale, that it was never meant to be sold. And now, as though confirming her belief, fate was giving her another chance to make sure it wasn't! It was Emma who had answered the phone, and if Laura hadn't been curious enough to ask who her sister was talking to, she might have missed this golden opportunity, she thought as she sat now curled up on her bed, hugging herself with excitement.

'Someone from Armstrong & McNulty.....or something like that,' was Emma's vague explanation.

Instantly Laura realised she meant Anderson & McCauley — the estate agents!

She almost snatched the receiver from her sister, who didn't even seem to notice in her hurry to get back to the television programme she'd been watching.

Explaining that her parents were out, Laura listened as the man on the other end of the line informed her there'd been a mix up in some arrangements which had been made for prospective buyers to view the Andrews property the following night.

'Unfortunately, my secretary double booked me and I'm already down to show some clients around another house at the same time. I'm afraid there's no one else available to stand in for me either,' the man said apologetically. 'We're extremely busy at the moment and I was wondering if your Mother or Father could, perhaps, on this occasion show the two couples around themselves? It would get me out of rather a mess.'

Without even having to think about it, Laura assured him there'd be no problem, and quickly made a note of the times for which the appointments had been made.

'I'm extremely grateful,' the estate agent said before ringing off.

'And so am I,' Laura thought as she replaced the receiver at her end.

Memorising the appointment times, she tore the piece of paper on which she'd written them into small pieces and put it the waste bin. She'd no intention of telling her parents about the phone call. She'd her own plans for tomorrow night. She knew that lying to people over the phone was one thing, she'd already proved she could do that. But lying to someone face to face was another matter entirely. She wasn't sure she'd manage that quite so easily, and certainly not on her own. She'd need help tomorrow night if she was going to be able to carry things off and there was only one person she could turn to for that.

"Success! Aishling has agreed to help. At the start she was pretty reluctant to get involved and took quite a bit of persuading. I kept telling her that preventing 'Rosemount' from being sold was the only way I could manage to get Auntie M back home again with the family, that there's no way Mum and Dad can keep up the payments if it isn't sold. But up until lunchtime she still hadn't agreed. Then halfway through our maths class this afternoon she passed me a note saying she'd come along tonight. I can hardly wait to get the whole thing over and done with. I'm shaking already at the thought, but I've just got to see it through. It's probably the last chance I'll get and I just can't let 'Rosemount' go without a fight."

Drawing aside the lace curtain just a fraction, Laura watched as the middle-aged couple closed the gate behind them. The woman glanced back towards the bungalow as the man opened the door of the car for her, and said something to him, a disappointed look on her face.

'Well, let's hope the next pair are as easy to fool,' Laura said as the car started up and pulled away.

'You know, we really shouldn't be doing this,' Aishling spoke from behind her.

'I know, I know,' Laura said wearily as she fixed the curtain back in place. 'But I have to try. If they manage to sell the place, Auntie M will be in Milton House for the rest of her days'.

'But what if we're found out? My parents would kill me if they knew I was doing something like this.'

Even as she spoke, Aishling knew she should have thought of all this earlier in the day when Laura had persuaded her to come along tonight. She was dressed now in a long loose jumper and multi-coloured leggings which she'd sneaked out of her older sister's wardrobe just before she'd left. She'd also managed to get her hands on a pair of long dangling earrings, a half-used tube of lipstick and some dark makeup and, now wearing all three, with her normally loose brown hair caught back behind her ears in two fashionable clips, she looked nearer to eighteen than her fourteen years as she acted out the part of Laura's older sister in this nerve-wracking conspiracy.

Seeing the worried look on Aishling's face, Laura said

'I'm sorry, Aishling. I suppose I shouldn't have involved you, but I just didn't think I'd be able to do it on my own. I'm really sorry…'

The sound of another car made Laura stop short, and again she went to the curtain and peered out.

'They're here.' For some strange reason, Laura found herself whispering although she and Aishling were the only two in the house.

A smart young couple stepped out of a red sports car and, immediately, the dark-haired elegantly dressed woman made her way purposely towards the house, without even waiting for her companion as he bent to lock the car doors. Even though the two friends were waiting for her to ring the doorbell, they jumped nervously when the shrill sound came.

'Ready?' Laura looked anxiously at Aishling.

Aishling nodded, glancing into the hall mirror, checking that her lipstick wasn't smudged and her make-up was still intact before opening the door.

'We're expected. Marshall's the name,' the woman said briskly, stepping into the hall and looking around her before Aishling had time to say a word. 'My husband,' she went on, indicating the man who just then arrived at the door. Aishling smiled shyly at him and taking a deep breath said in a rush,

'I'm sorry. I know you were expecting my Mother to be here, but she wasn't able to make it tonight. Something unexpected came up.'

'Damn!' the woman said. 'But surely that doesn't mean we can't have a look around the place. You're both here, after all.' She looked from Aishling to Laura.

'Oh, yes, of course, but there's something else...'

'Yes?' The man spoke for the first time.

'Well, my sister and I have already shown another couple around just before you, and they've decided to buy.'

'Damn.' The woman seemed fond of the word. 'A wasted journey then,' she said turning to her husband her expression displeased.

'Maybe not. You never know, they may have second thoughts. Might as well have a look around while we're here, darling,' he suggested.

Aishling glanced at Laura. Things were taking a different turn this time. When she'd told the middle-aged couple that the bungalow was already sold, they'd simply expressed their disappointment and left. It didn't look as though these people were going to be as easy to get rid of.

'Any problem with that?' Mr Marshall asked.

'Sorry?' Aishling said.

'Looking around.'

The man looked hard at her and Aishling wondered if he knew she was lying. For a second she couldn't answer, but coming to her rescue Laura said brightly,

'Of course not. You're very welcome to look the place over. Take as long as you like.'

The Marshalls took Laura at her word and half an hour later were still there. The two friends sat in the living room, hardly speaking and only in whispers when they did. They could hear the woman's voice from the end of the corridor which led to the bedrooms as she remarked on the various built-in wardrobes and the size of the rooms.

At last they were ready to leave.

'Lovely. Lovely house altogether,' the Marshall woman enthused as, hearing her approach, the girls came out of the living room to join her and her husband in the hall.

'Yes, isn't it,' Laura agreed.

'Pity about it already being sold. Please tell your parents that if there's any hitch with the other people to be sure to have the estate agents get in touch with us. We're very interested in buying, too.'

'I will,' Aishling promised.

'I don't think there's much chance of them changing their minds, do you?' Laura butted in, giving her 'older sister' a nudge. 'They seemed very definite about things when they left,' she added, her tone oozing confidence.

'Well, you never know, you never know,' Mr. Marshall said as he stood, hands in his trouser pockets, patiently waiting while his wife had yet another look around the living-room.

'Right,' she said briskly when she'd seen all she wanted. Then bidding the girls goodnight, the couple left.

'Phew, that was hard work,' Aishling said as the sports car sped away.

'D'you think they were convinced?' Laura wondered.

'I'm not sure. Probably. After all, they'd no reason not to believe us.'

'Suppose you're right.' Laura stood there looking at her friend for reassurance. Now that the Marshalls had left, her air of confidence was quickly deserting her. Just then the grandfather clock in the hall began to chime.

'Gosh! Half past nine! We'd better get going. I said I'd be home by now,' Aishling exclaimed.

'I've got to make that phone call first, remember? Don't want the estate agent ringing Mum first thing in the morning to see how she got on with his clients. We'd really be in for it then,' Laura said with a light-heartedness she didn't feel.

'Well, while you're making the call, I'd better get changed out of these clothes and wash off this make-up. I don't think it's exactly how my parents would expect me to look coming home from badminton practice!' Aishling grimaced.

Laura dialled Anderson & McCauley's number. At this hour, she knew it was most unlikely there'd be anyone there and suspected she'd only get an answering service. She was relieved when she heard the recorded message, feeling drained now after the efforts of the evening and glad to find she only had to deal with a machine and not some suave, high-powered sales person. As soon as she heard the bleep, choosing her words carefully, she gave her Mother's name and left a message that neither couple had been in the least interested in purchasing her aunt's property!

Making sure the burglar alarm was switched on and all windows and doors locked, the two girls set off. They cycled home, hardly speaking. Laura knew Aishling was upset at what they'd just done. She felt extremely guilty now at involving the other girl. Things were different for her — she had Auntie M to think of, and because of that the risk of what would happen if they were ever found out, was worth it. But Aishling had nothing to gain from what they'd done, and for that reason alone, Laura prayed silently as they rode along that tonight's activities would go undiscovered. When they reached the corner where Aishling turned off, Laura said 'Well...see you tomorrow, then.'

Her friend nodded.

'And, Aishling,' Laura leaned over and touched her on the arm, '...thanks.'

Then two friends cycled off in opposite directions.

Three days passed.

There were no further phone calls from the estate agents and no other prospective buyers appeared on the scene.

'It's a bad time to be selling,' Tom Phelan told his wife. 'There's not all that much money floating around these days, with almost three hundred thousand unemployed in this little country of ours, you know. People are holding onto what they've got. If they have a home already they're staying put.'

'Still, you'd think there'd be someone interested,' his wife said doubtfully.

'There will be, Marge, there will be. It'll just take time'.

After a week had passed Laura found herself beginning to relax. They'd managed to get away with it. And also, equally important, was the fact that 'Rosemount' still hadn't been sold!

And then it happened.

The Marshalls contacted Anderson & McCauley!

'But, I tell you I never got the message,' Marjorie Phelan told the estate agent adamantly when he rang. 'I've never even heard of a Mr and Mrs Marshall. And you say my daughter took the call? Are you absolutely certain?'

The man from Anderson & McCauley was absolutely certain. Not only did he assure Laura's Mother that the Marshalls did exist but that they'd actually been to see her Aunt's bungalow and, what's more, were extremely interested in buying it. And the strangest thing of all was, that he insisted they'd been shown around by her two teenage daughters! Two teenagers certainly ruled out Emma being involved, Marjorie Phelan decided, apart from the fact that she'd been in all that night watching one of her favourite TV programmes. But Laura had been out — she'd had badminton practise that particular evening. Or so she'd said…But, if one of the teenage girls had been Laura, then who on earth was the other?

Still confused about the whole thing, she said into the phone 'Look, I'll have a word with my older daughter when she gets in from school. In the meantime, would you please explain to the Marshalls that there has obviously been some sort of mix up and that the bungalow is most definitely still for sale.'

As soon as Laura turned the key in the hall door, she heard her Mother's voice from the kitchen.

'Laura, I'd like a word with you.'

'I'm just going to put my things upstairs,' Laura answered.

'Now, please, Laura, if it's not too much trouble. This can't wait,' her Mother said from where she now stood framed in the kitchen door.

Before her Mother, who was looking unusually stern-faced, said one more word, Laura guessed what had happened. And before her daughter could even deny what she was about to ask, Marjorie Phelan knew she'd been involved in whatever conspiracy had taken place. The look of guilt on Laura's face told its own story.

'To think you'd do such a thing, Laura. I can't believe it. I'm so ashamed of you,' she said when she'd finally managed to get the whole story out of her. And then, almost as if she was talking to herself she went on, 'and to involve Aishling, too. That was completely unfair — using a friend like that.'

Her initial anger now almost spent, Marjorie Phelan found herself on the verge of tears as she thought of all that had been going on behind her back. Not only had Laura planned the episode of over a week ago with the Marshalls, but she'd lied about there being no phone calls in response to the newspaper advertisement, too. Lashing back angrily at her Mother's accusations, Laura had denied nothing and had even seemed proud to tell of all the terrible things she'd done. Unable to hold them back any longer, Marjorie Phelan now burst into tears. Her fair-haired daughter stood watching her for a second or two, contempt written all over her face, her green eyes scornful as she turned away.

"We've both been grounded for the next two weeks. Except for when we meet up at school, Aishling and I are forbidden to 'communicate'. (Dad's word). That means no half-day get-togethers and definitely no phone calls.'

Mum is very quiet, and every time I come face to face with Dad it's like I've stepped inside the Arctic circle! Well, I did what I did and I'm not sorry. I am sorry for Aishling though, for getting her into all this trouble. But at least 'Rosemount' isn't sold yet."

But , despite all Laura's efforts to ignore it, as the days passed she soon found herself having to face up to the harsh fact that the sale of the bungalow was in its final stages and that within a very short time the Marshalls would be its new owners.

'Why don't you ever go to visit Auntie M?' Emma asked out of the blue one night.

What a stupid question, Laura thought, as she

looked across to where her sister lay in the other bed. To the disappointment of both girls, they were still sharing the same room, their parents having decided to redecorate Emma's before she moved back in. At first the two of them had thought it would be for only a matter of days. But their Mother, who, in Emma's opinion especially, had a 'thing' about matching everything, was still undecided as to which wallpaper went with which carpet, and, as a result, they found themselves still room-mates.

'More like cell-mates,' Laura thought to herself at times, now fed up with going to bed early each night. But anything was better than sitting downstairs looking at the television, and keeping up the 'terrible silence' as she called it. There was a time when she'd actually enjoyed sitting in looking at TV with her parents, but not these last weeks. Now she'd have gone out every night had she been allowed, but, of course, she wasn't. On top of everything else, she couldn't even ring Aishling any more until this stupid grounding period was over! So, with nothing else to do, most nights she simply went to bed and read.

'Well?' Emma spoke again.

'Well what?' Laura asked grumpily.

'Why don't you ever go to see Auntie M?'

'If you don't understand by now, Stupid, then you never will.'

'Try me,' Emma invited.

But Laura turned over onto her side and continued reading, refusing to say any more.

Emma opened her own book but didn't immediately begin to read. Laura's behaviour puzzled her.

How could anyone who'd been so fond of someone, just as her sister had been of Auntie M, suddenly cut them out of their life completely? As far as Emma could see, that was what Laura had done and she found it impossible to understand why. Her confusion about the whole thing was what had prompted her question. Why was her sister behaving the way she was? She knew, of course, that Laura had never wanted their Great-aunt to go into the nursing home in the first place, but now that she was there, why wouldn't Laura go to visit? She'd gone a few times with her parents and from what she could see it was a lovely place and their aunt seemed happy there. And she really enjoyed the weekly bingo sessions. She'd told Emma that, and of how one of the nurses had helped her mark her card. She'd even won a small prize one night! Next time she won something she'd promised she'd keep it for her. So why wouldn't Laura visit? Emma knew she refused flatly every time their Mother suggested it, and these days her sister never mentioned their Great-aunt's name. Certainly not to her anyway. She still hadn't got over her surprise at what Laura and Aishling Dalton had done. She'd never have guessed they'd have the nerve. Secretly, she thought the whole episode must have been quite exciting. She and Laura had never been really close, but she had to admit that Laura had always been OK to her, and quite the opposite of the snappy, moody person she'd become in the last few months. She was her only sister, after all, Emma reasoned as she lay there, and if Laura was really as unhappy as she now appeared, then she was prepared to help if she could...

'Laura,' she ventured.

'What?' her sister snapped.

'I was just thinking…'

'Thinking!' The word was loaded with sarcasm.

'Ah, forget it.' Rebuffed, Emma decided if that was the attitude Laura was going to take, it would probably be best to leave her to sort out her own problems. And the sooner her room was ready to move back into the better it would be for both of them.

"Emma really caught me off guard last night with her questions. If she only knew just how much I'd love to see Auntie M. I have to hold myself back every time the rest of them are going to visit her. I miss her so much and I think about her every day. From what I can make out, she seems to have settled in reasonably well, but I'd like to hear it from her… I could write to her, but she wouldn't be able to reply. Unless of course she got one of the other residents to do it for her — and that wouldn't be the same. I've thought about ringing her, but I know it would be impossible to understand what she was saying over the phone. There seems to be no way of making contact with her apart from going to see her in "that place". But doing that would be like giving in, like saying everything is OK and that it was alright to send her there in the first place… Well, it wasn't."

CHAPTER TWELVE

'Look at the size of the place,' Marie O'Neill said as the mini bus pulled into the parking area. 'It's huge!'

Aishling, Laura and Phil Brennan, who, with Marie made up the 'B' team, peered out the window.

'Phew,' Phil said, giving an appreciative whistle as she took in the large modern building 'Some leisure complex!'

Even Laura, who today seemed quieter than ever, had to admit that the place looked impressive.

'Now, don't let the size of this place faze you,' Deirdre O'Brien said, knowing that when they went inside the girls would be even more impressed. She remembered her own surprise the first time she'd stepped into the complex's vast badminton hall. There were ten courts in all and compared to the two-court hall which the girls were used to for practice, the place would seem enormous.

In the changing rooms there was a buzz of excitement. Coaches chatted and introduced teams to each other, as girls hurriedly changed from track suits to badminton skirts and tops, and laced up the latest in sports shoes.

'This is it, girls. The day we've all been working towards,' their coach said, as she grouped them together before they headed out to start their matches. Remember to keep your concentration, and, don't forget, no matter how many points you may be leading by, you must never become complacent. Keep fighting to stay ahead. Things sometimes have a way of turning around and no team can afford to feel they've won until the last point has been scored.'

The four of them nodded.

'Now get out there and show them what you're made of,' she said, finishing up with what the girls called her Jack Charlton line.

Because it was the final, quite a number of the team's supporters had come to cheer them on. The home teams had their followers, too, and when Laura and Aishling walked into the huge hall, they found quite a sizeable crowd of excited spectators impatiently waiting for the finals to commence.

'Fame at last,' Aishling joked as a cheer went up from one corner and they looked across to see several of their classmates waving school scarves.

'Better not let that lot down,' Laura said as they began their warm up. Aishling hoped Laura would be able to stand the pace, noticing how pale her friend looked. The other finalists had won the championships last year and she knew it wasn't going to be easy to take their title away from them. She'd seen Laura shiver slightly earlier in the changing room, even though it was a warm day, and she'd noticed, too, that a couple of times she'd rubbed her stomach as though she was in some sort of pain. Aishling had decided to say nothing, remembering that on the last occasion Laura had explained away her stomach cramps as being due to nerves. And who wouldn't be nervous on a day like today, Aishling thought, as she moved around the court trying to ease away some of the tension which had built up in her own muscles.

'Laura, Aishling. Laura, Aishling,' their supporters chanted after they'd won the first match. But the second game, as far as Aishling was concerned, was the hardest she'd ever played — and lost — making the score one match each after three quarters of an hour of play.

Laura's forehead was damp with perspiration. She looked as white as a ghost and during the short interval before the final game, Aishling watched her anxiously as she gulped down a glass of water.

'Tired, Laura?'

'No.' Laura's reply was terse as she looked sharply at her team-mate. 'Should I be?'

'No, no. I just wondered. Feeling a bit puffed myself, that's all,' Aishling said with forced cheerfulness, wanting to avoid conflict at all costs, knowing that everything depended now on the game yet to be played.

As she waited for the signal to go back on court, Laura silently admitted to herself that she felt terrible. She hadn't really been feeling well for days. She regretted now that she'd answered Aishling so sharply, but she hadn't wanted to be reminded of how badly she was feeling right now. Somehow, she'd managed to carry on this far. But she knew that if she once began to think of how much her stomach was aching, and gave in to the slightly dizzy feeling in her head, she wouldn't be able to keep on playing.

She couldn't bear sympathy at the moment, not even Aishling's. Concentrate — that was what she needed to do now — to concentrate on one thing and that was giving the next and final game everything she'd got.

A sudden huge cheer from the far end of the hall, and the look on the faces of Marie and Phil, told her that the 'B' team had been successful. Now it was up to her and Aishling to go out there and make it a double. Wiping her face and hands in a towel, she picked up her racquet and once again took her place beside Aishling as the umpire announced that the third game was about to commence.

Like the shuttlecock, the leading score passed from one side of the net to the other, leaving very little between either team. The atmosphere was tense throughout the huge hall, with both sets of supporters not daring to take their eyes off play for even a second. Knowing they had to do something to gain, and hold onto, a decent lead, Aishling made a pre-arranged signal to Laura that she was about to try a very short serve. She was hoping to catch the other team — who were now beginning to show signs of tiredness — off their guard. Laura took a few steps towards the back of the court, leaving the front clear for Aishling in the event of a return shot landing just over the net. If , by some chance, it travelled towards the back of the court, then she'd be properly positioned to handle whatever came her way. But the service wasn't returned and, to the delight of their supporters, Aishling went on to score three more points in quick succession. Realising they'd lost control of the match, no matter what the other team did they seemed unable to score again even when they had the opportunity, and within minutes the final game of the interschool's badminton championships had come to an end. Laura and Aishling had done it! They'd won!

Their supporters crowded onto the court and, amid all the cheering and hugging, the two team-mates became separated. Both of them were lifted shoulder high and dozens of familiar school faces grinned up at them as they were carried around the huge hall, with Aishling clinging tightly to the gleaming silver trophy, just about managing not to drop it. It was only when some of the excitement had died down a little and Aishling found herself safely back on the ground that she caught sight of her friend again. Laura was leaning against the wall, her hand to her forehead, her face ashen. As she disentangled herself from a group of delighted classmates and hurried over to see what was the matter, Laura slumped down onto the floor.

'Keep back. Give her some air,' Aishling said as dozens of girls began to crowd around. 'And somebody tell Ms O'Brien. Call her over, will you? She's at the other end of the hall.'

Deirdre O'Brien arrived within seconds. 'Stand back, stand back, girls. Give her some air,' she said, repeating Aishling's earlier request, as she made her way through the crowd.

'What happened?'

'I don't know. I saw her leaning against the wall and then she just slid down onto the floor.' Aishling looked again at Laura's still form and white face. Her expression anxious, she turned to their coach for reassurance.

'Laura, Laura.' Deirdre O'Brien spoke firmly, tapping Laura gently on the side of her face as she spoke. 'Wake up, Laura. Come on now, wake up.'

Slowly Laura opened her eyes. They widened in surprise as she looked into the sea of faces staring down at her. She made an unsteady attempt to get up but was quickly stopped by her coach.

'Easy. Take it easy, Laura,' she warned, putting her hand on the young girls shoulder. 'Don't try to get up just yet. Wait until you're ready.' Turning to a girl on her left, she asked 'Will you bring her a drink of water, please?' And then to the group as a whole suggested, 'I think the rest of you should head off home now. Don't worry, we'll see that she's alright.'

There were murmurs of 'See you, Laura', 'Congrats' and 'take care,' as the crowd of friends and supporters slowly broke up and drifted away.

The minibus came to a halt outside the Phelan's house.

'No, no. I'll come in with you,' Deirdre O'Brien insisted when Laura said she'd rather go in alone. She'd noticed that the girl had tried to make very light of what had happened and Deirdre O'Brien was convinced that she'd no intention of telling her Mother about it either. And she didn't think that would be a very good idea. Laura had taken quite a bit of time to come round and when they'd finally got her to her feet, she'd swayed unsteadily and had needed help in making her way to the minibus. No, it was best if she went in with her, her coach decided, as she climbed down out of the vehicle onto the pavement and held up her hand to assist her young charge. In her opinion, Laura's collapse had been more than just a fainting attack. The girl was ill and needed to be seen by a doctor. She felt it was her duty to make sure that Mrs Phelan knew exactly what had happened to her daughter this afternoon.

CHAPTER THIRTEEN

Dr Nolan, a brisk man in his early sixties, had been the Phelan's family doctor for years. He headed up the stairs now followed by Laura's mother who, speaking softly, filled him in on what had happened.

'Let's have a look at you then, shall we, young lady? Might as well find out what all the fuss is about. Right?' he said, taking in Laura's wax-like pallor.

Raising her up in the bed, Dr Nolan blew on his stetascope before placing it first on Laura's chest and then on her back, all the time listening intently. Then asking her to lie down, he pulled back the bedclothes and began to gently examine her abdomen. The doctor nodded occasionally as his fingers pressed deeply on various parts of his young patient's stomach. When he finished, he asked Laura to sit out on the side of the bed and, one at a time, he gave each of her knees a sharp tap as he tested her reflexes. Then telling her that she could get back in he turned to her Mother and said 'Marjorie, I'd like to have a word with your daughter alone for a moment, if you've no objections.'

'Of course not. I'll be right outside.'

On the landing, Laura's mother could hear the low murmur of their voices coming from inside the room. She prayed there was nothing seriously wrong. So far in her young life, Laura had been lucky enough to have had little more than a heavy cold. This fainting business was so unlike her, she thought as the door opened and Dr Nolan came out. The expression on his face was serious and she looked anxiously at him as she waited to hear what he had to say.

After the doctor had gone, Marjorie Phelan went straight to the kitchen, put on the kettle and made herself a cup of strong tea. She needed time to think before she could face Laura. Why hadn't she taken more notice when morning after morning she'd pushed aside her breakfast and refused to eat hardly anything. But, then she hadn't exactly been glowing herself in the mornings these past weeks. She'd been completely taken up, too, with looking after Auntie M and had been far too busy to pay attention to anything else.

'The child's been blaming herself for what happened to your aunt,' Dr. Nolan had explained. 'Oh, she didn't say it in so many words, Marjorie,' he said a little more gently, seeing the shocked look on her face. 'And it's not that she doesn't want to eat. It seems that her stomach is constantly in a knot, worrying about what's happened and she just can't seem to swallow her food. She described it as that awful feeling she sometimes gets before an exam.'

'Blaming herself? But how could she think she had anything to do with Auntie M becoming ill?' Marjorie Phelan had asked in disbelief.

'I tried explaining that to her. I told her that her aunt had been attending me with high blood pressure for some time before her stroke. I said I'd warned the woman not to do anything too strenuous, but would she listen? No. It probably would have happened anyway if she'd kept up her usual lifestyle. Cutting grass or not cutting grass! But I don't think I convinced Laura. And then there's the added fact that your aunt's in a nursing home now. That's playing on her mind too.'

'Poor Laura. What do you think I should do, Doctor?' her Mother asked.

'Well, I know you've been under a lot of strain yourself this past while, Marjorie, but I'm afraid that sometimes we adults tend to forget that young people, too, can suffer from stress. Laura seems to have had her fair share of it lately, so I suggest a day or two in bed won't do her any harm. Maybe some of her favourite dishes might just tempt her to eat a bit more. But, you know, my dear, my advice to you is that now is the time to tell her what's really going on.'

Sipping her tea, Laura's mother mused over the doctor's parting words, yet somehow she wasn't quite convinced this was the moment to impart her news, not with her daughter as weak as she was just now. But it had to be done soon, she knew that. Perhaps in a few days when Laura was a little stronger she'd finally find the opportunity she'd been waiting for during these past weeks.

'Isn't it gorgeous?' Aishling waltzed around the bedroom, the huge silver trophy clutched tightly to her chest.

Marie O'Neill and Phil Brennan, between them holding their slightly smaller cup, laughed. The three of them had called to see how Laura was feeling after her collapse of the day before.

'We had to do a tour of the school with them today,' Aishling said to Laura as she rubbed a finger mark off the cup with the cuff of her jumper. 'Even old "Ms X-squared" was impressed,' she went on, referring to their maths teacher. 'She actually let us off homework for this afternoon! Here — have a proper look at it,' she said, and holding out the gleaming trophy offered it to Laura. 'You didn't get a chance to yesterday, what with that great passing-out act you performed.' Aishling smiled impishly as she spoke, winking at the other two, as she waited for Laura to take the cup from her. But to her disappointment, Laura only touched it lightly with her hand and didn't seem at all interested in a closer inspection. She seems so tired, Aishling thought as she saw her friend slump back against the pillows.

'Better go then, I suppose,' she said turning to the others.

'Yeah, suppose so,' agreed Phil.

'See you then, Laura,' Marie said.

'Yeah, see you, Laura,' Aishling and Phil echoed.

But their friend's only acknowledgement of their going was a limp wave of her hand.

"Mum sits watching me every time she brings me something to eat. I can almost see her counting the mouthfuls. I do try to eat, but as soon as I think about all that's happened, of Auntie M no longer living at 'Rosemount', but instead stuck in that awful place and of not being able to see her whenever I want, my stomach just seems to seize up and the cramps start all over again.

Mum's always going on about eating more, saying that all she and Dad want is for me to get better! She even said Emma was going around with a long face these days. I'll bet!! And today she brought Auntie M into it, saying she's always asking about me and wondering when I'm going to visit her. Well, using that line is definitely not going to win me around."

After three or four days, Laura was still looking pale and sad. Worrying about her daughter's unhappiness, and not knowing what else to do Marjorie Phelan once again decided to call on Dr. Nolan. This time she remained in the room as he spoke to her daughter.

'Laura, child,' he said gently, as he sat on the edge of her bed, 'you've got to give up this battle. You can't keep on blaming yourself for what happened to your aunt, and you can't keep on blaming your Mother because she couldn't continue to care for her here. There comes a time in almost everyone's life, you know, when they have to make difficult decisions. And your aunt moving into Milton House has probably been the most difficult one your Mother has had to make so far. You're not the only one who's suffered because of it, Laura. Your Mother has suffered, too, and, I have absolutely no doubt, so has your aunt. But, she at least understood that it had to happen. And that's what you've got to try to do — understand your Mother's position, child.

I've known both your aunt and your Mother for

years, Laura, and I know they thought the world of each other, and still do. Your Mother had a very good reason for doing what she did and I've made her promise to tell you exactly what it is as soon as I've left. Perhaps she should have told you before now, but she had her own reasons for not doing so. But I'm sure you'll see things very differently when you hear what she has to say.'

Picking up his bag, Dr. Nolan added 'Think about what I've said, will you? And remember, your Mother and I only want what's best for you.'

At his final words, Laura's Mother saw her daughter stiffen in the bed.

As the door closed after him, Laura fought back angry tears. So, it seemed her Mother had won him over to her way of thinking, too. She 'thought the world' of her aunt! How could the stupid man believe that when she'd been happy to give up looking after her. She'd 'a very good reason' for what she'd done — he believed that, too!! Despite herself Laura almost laughed. She was sick of all their lies, of listening to the same thing over and over and over. She was tired, too. Tired of feeling so weak, tired of always being filled with anger. Sometimes she wanted so badly to believe that her Mother had acted for the best. She missed the happy, loving relationship they used to have. Sometimes she wanted to simply forget about the whole thing, to pretend it just hadn't happened, to have things back the way they used to be. But there was always a part of her which wouldn't give in, a part of her which still refused to be convinced. Well, Laura thought bitterly, hope she doesn't delay too long in seeing the old fool out because I just can't wait to hear what this very good reason is!

CHAPTER FOURTEEN

'Laura.'

Marjorie Phelan opened the bedroom door cautiously as though half-expecting to be met with an avalanche of abuse of some sort or another. Instead she found her daughter lying back against the headboard, the bedclothes pulled up defensively as far as her chin. She stood for a moment — silent, not knowing where to begin — before sitting down on the edge of the bed. She looked at the pale face, the tightly clenched lips, wondering anxiously how Laura would react to what she was about to tell her. Aware of her Mother's scrutiny, Laura turned her head away. It was then that Marjorie Phelan knew there was no use easing into an explanation about why she'd acted this way or that. Shock tactics were needed! So, clearing her throat, she said,

'Laura, I'm pregnant. I'm going to have a baby.'

Laura slowly turned to face her. Her expression was one of complete and utter amazement. She lay staring at her Mother for what seemed an age and then said in a whisper 'A baby?'

Her Mother nodded.

'A baby,' Laura repeated and then, 'But you can't be. Not after...not at your...' She stopped, unable to put into words exactly what she wanted to say.

'After so many years, you mean? Or at my age?'

her Mother said, finishing for her.

'Well…yes, both,' Laura mumbled.

'I can assure you it's true, Laura. I know that Emma's twelve and it's a huge gap, but it's not all that unusual. Plenty of women have babies in their early forties…'

Marjorie Phelan paused, taking in her daughter's still dazed expression, before going on.

'So you see, now, Laura, why I couldn't continue caring for Auntie M. It was a choice between the two — her and the baby — a very difficult choice. And your Dad and I felt the baby had to come first. I had to face the fact that Auntie M had had a full and healthy life for well into her seventies. Still, it broke my heart to send her to Milton House. But if I'd continued running up and down stairs, and had kept on doing all the other things she needed to make her comfortable, sadly this little baby wouldn't have stood a chance.'

Laura watched her Mother gently pat her stomach as she spoke.

'Does she know?' Laura asked.

'Auntie M, you mean? Yes, but only for the last week or so. I didn't tell her earlier because I thought if she knew she'd feel she had to leave here even sooner and I wanted her to have as much time as possible to get used to the idea of going into the home. I also thought it would be a good idea to let her settle well into her new surroundings before saying anything.'

'What did she say?'

'She's happy if I'm happy, Laura,' her Mother told her and then 'Now that you know the reason for everything, you'll go to see her soon, won't you?'

Laura nodded and then asked 'Have you told anyone else?'

'Only your Uncle John and Aishling's Mother. But she was sworn to secrecy. I needed to know there was someone I could call on if things didn't work out.'

'Didn't work out?' Laura's tone was puzzled.

'Yes. Anything could have happened, Laura. That's why I didn't tell you before now. I was afraid…'

'Afraid?' Laura looked enquiringly at her Mother, her tone even more puzzled this time.

'Afraid of losing the baby…afraid of disappointing you and Emma…' Marjorie Phelan paused for a moment before continuing. 'You were far too young at the time to understand what was going on, but when Emma was a little over a year old I had a miscarriage…and that almost happened again this time. So, you see, if I'd told you and Emma too soon, and things hadn't worked out and there was no new brother or sister at the end of it all…'

'Was that what was wrong when you said you had a tummy bug?'

'Yes.'

'And it's because of the baby you're redecorating Emma's room?'

'Yes.'

'I see.'

Not appearing to have any more questions, Laura lay back, staring into space. Marjorie Phelan sat watching her daughter, waiting for her reaction to what she'd been told. Studying her, she found her expression told her nothing, her thoughts impossible to read. Then, after a moment or two, she asked softly, 'What about you, Laura? What do you think of the news?'

Laura pursed her lips.

'It's OK…I suppose.'

It wasn't exactly the answer her Mother had been hoping for, but she said nothing. At least Laura had agreed to visit Milton House. For that much, at least, she was grateful.

"Well, at least now I know why Mum acted as she did. I suppose I've got to accept the fact that she hadn't much choice and that looking after us and Auntie M and a baby would be a pretty impossible task, but PREGNANT — at fortysomething. How could she? I couldn't come straight out and say it, but I think she guessed I wasn't exactly overjoyed at the news.

Gosh! How am I going to face Aishling and the rest of the gang at school? Even if I say nothing, they're going to find out eventually. It'll be all so embarrassing. Nobody, but nobody in my year has anyone under the age of ten in their family! Imagine — I'll be twenty-four when the baby's that age! I'll be more like a Mother than a sister! Talking of sisters, wonder what Emma will say. Knowing her, she probably won't bat an eyelid. And Auntie M? Was she being honest when she told Mum she was happy if Mum was. Wonder what she really thinks, how she really is? Can't wait to see her…"

EPILOGUE

The grounds of Milton House were deserted. Unlike the afternoon of Laura's first visit there, on this occasion the weather had decided to be inhospitable and grey, blustery clouds scurried across the sky. But Laura hardly noticed as, accompanied by her Mother, she hurried up the steps and quickly rang the bell. The same pleasant-faced woman, whom she now knew to be called Mrs. Sweeney, opened the door to them.

'Mrs Andrews is in the day-room,' she told Laura's Mother as they stepped inside.

'I'm sure you'd like a few minutes on your own with Auntie M first. I'll wait down here for a while,' Marjorie Phelan said tactfully to her daughter, taking a seat in the entrance hall. The words were no sooner out of her mouth than Laura was gone. She hurried along the corridor and up the wide staircase. Even if she hadn't known where the day-room was, the buzz of chatter coming from it would have led her in the right direction.

She stood in the doorway for a moment, looking around the room. And then, just to the right of the fireplace she saw her. Auntie M was sitting between two other grey-haired companions, smiling at something which one of them had said. As though sensing she was being watched, she turned her head and looked in Laura's direction. At the sight of her Great-niece, for a second a look of disbelief flashed across her face and then, as she realised she wasn't seeing things, she extended her 'good arm' in welcome.

Laura pulled her chair even closer, if that was possible, to her Great-aunt's. Although she found that her speech had improved, it was still somewhat unclear and she didn't want to miss a word of what she had to say. Now comfortably settled in the privacy of her Great-aunt's room, they talked and talked, oblivious of the time and were amazed to find that more than an hour had flown by when Marjorie Phelan finally gave a gentle knock on the door.

"Everything about today was brilliant!

I couldn't believe Auntie M looked so well. She's made lots of new friends and seems to be really happy at Milton. She's got her own T.V. and video in her room and the Matron even organised a book prop stand for her, so she doesn't get tired holding her book in one hand all the time. Now all she's got to do is turn the page!

She didn't seem a bit angry that I hadn't come to see her sooner. And that was something that was really worrying me. She wanted to know all about school and, of course, winning the badminton championships.

And we talked for ages about the baby.

She understood exactly how I feel about it all — that it's more Mum being pregnant that I find hard to take, than the idea of having a baby in the house. But she says that in the end most of my friends will probably envy me, because almost everyone loves a baby. Yet pushing it around in its pram — I can't really see myself doing that! Although Auntie M says that I may even find myself wanting to at some stage! Especially, she said, if it's as pretty as she remembers me being when I was small. However, I'm not convinced! But, still, I've never known her to be wrong about anything yet. Strangely enough, after talking it through, I don't feel half so bad about it all now.

The most exciting thing she told me was that Mum has promised that after the baby's born, and she's got her strength back, she'll arrange to take Auntie M home for visits! Wouldn't that really be something!

After not seeing her for so long, I was scared she'd be different, somehow.

But she's not.

And, you know something, I can still talk to her about anything!"

THE END

THE BRIGHT SPARKS FAN CLUB
WOULD YOU LIKE TO JOIN?

You are already half way there. If you fill in the questionnaire on the reverse side of this page and one other questionnaire from any of the other **BRIGHT SPARKS** titles and return both questionnaires to **Attic Press** at the address below, you automatically become a member of the **BRIGHT SPARKS FAN CLUB**.

If you are, like many others, a lover of the **BRIGHT SPARKS** fiction series and become a member of the **BRIGHT SPARKS FAN CLUB**, you will receive special discount offers on all new **BRIGHT SPARKS** books, plus receive a **BRIGHT SPARKS** bookmark and a beautiful friendship braclet made with the **BRIGHT SPARKS** colours. Traditionally friendship braclets are worn by friends until they fall off! If your friends would like to join the club, tell them to buy the books and become a member of this book lovers club.

Please keep on reading and spread the word about our wonderful books. We look forward to hearing from you soon.

Name _____

Address _____

_____

You can order your books by post, fax and phone direct from:
Attic Press, 4 Upper Mount St, Dublin 2. Ireland.
Tel: (01) 6616 128 Fax: (01) 6616 176

The *BRIGHT SPARKS*
Questionnaire and Fan Club

Attic Press hopes you enjoyed **A Very Good Reason**.
To help us improve the **BRIGHT SPARKS** series for
you please answer the following questions.

1. Why did you decide to buy this book?

_____
_____
_____

2. Did you enjoy this book? Why?

_____
_____
_____

3. Where did you buy it?

_____
_____
_____

4. What do you think of the cover?

_____
_____
_____

4. Have you ever read any other books in the **BRIGHT
SPARKS** series? Which one/s?

_____
_____
_____

If there is not enough space for your answers on this coupon
continue on a sheet of paper and attach it to the coupon.

Post this coupon to **Attic Press**, 4 Upper Mount Street,
Dublin 2 and we'll send you a **BRIGHT SPARKS**
bookmark, or fill in two questionnaires from two **BRIGHT
SPARKS** books and become a member of the *BRIGHT
SPARKS FAN CLUB*. See reverse side for details.

Name _____
Address _____
_____

You can order your books by post, fax and phone direct from:
Attic Press, 4 Upper Mount St, Dublin 2. Ireland.
Tel: (01) 6616 128 Fax: (01) 6616 176